Dear Reader,

His Kind of Woman was my first published book and is very special to my heart. It won the Romance Writers of America's Golden Heart Award. I hope the humor, sensual sparks and small-town atmosphere I encountered as I reread *His Kind of Woman* will touch your hearts and lift your spirits. You'll probably notice that this book was written in an earlier age of innocence, before extreme violence found its way into American elementary schools. The words with which this story is told reflect the once-held belief that the most traumatic event a ten-year-old boy could experience at school would be being disciplined by the principal for unleashing a pack of renegade frogs in the auditorium—said principal being the boy's mother.

Pat Tracy

PAT TRACY

still lives in Idaho. A woman's life can change a lot in twelve years. Hers has. But she still believes in old-fashioned values, true love and the power of homemade apple dumplings to change fate.

Books by Pat Tracy

Silhouette Romance

His Kind of Woman #654
Tiger by the Tail #710
Sherman's Surrender #828
Wild Streak #887

Harlequin Historical

The Flaming #121
Winter Fire #188
Saddle the Wind #273
Beloved Outcast #333
Cade's Justice #392
Burke's Rules #446
Hunter's Law #509

*The Guardsmen

Pat Tracy
His Kind of Woman

Silhouette Books

Published by Silhouette Books

America's Publisher of Contemporary Romance

Dedicated to:
Julie, Kristen and Sheriann—
my lovely daughters and most loyal fans
And to:
Karen, Sherry, Maxine, Peggy,
Linda, Janie, Sandra, Jackie and Charlu—
fellow writers who generously shared
their time, advice and encouragement
And to:
Luann Simmons, for her special assistance

SILHOUETTE BOOKS

ISBN 0-373-82260-X

HIS KIND OF WOMAN

Visit Silhouette at www.eHarlequin.com

Printed in U.S.A.

Chapter One

Grace Banner strode purposefully toward the shop area of Hollister's Auto Repair, her heels clicking sharply against the concrete floor. She considered the handwritten sign that read Employees Only, and her gray eyes narrowed. She had no intention of letting a dusty cardboard sign keep her from talking to Matthew Hollister. He had put her off long enough.

She raised her hands and pushed open the swinging doors that led directly to the shop. Her momentum carried her into a steaming jungle of machine parts and intimidating tools. A wave of heat and the acid smell of machine oil engulfed her.

Three steps into the stifling room, Grace sighted the object of her manhunt sprawled upon the shop's green concrete floor. Or at any rate, the lower half of him, she amended, surveying the pair of long legs encased in faded denim that projected from beneath a brown station wagon. Scuffed leather work boots covered his feet.

For a moment Grace was caught off balance. So the rumors were true. This was how Blake's former political rival was spending his time—as a common laborer. Despite the rumors and the proof lying in front of her, Grace had trouble believing Matthew Hollister was really working in his father's repair shop. Even temporarily.

Too clearly etched in her memory was the high-powered corporate president drafted by his party to run against her late husband for the same Idaho congressional seat. A remnant of long-ago hostility surged within Grace. Even though her antagonism toward this man sprang from events ten years in the past, her feelings were still surprisingly raw.

Grace stared at the powerful male legs stretching out from beneath the car. Her fingers went to the delicate lace collar of her blouse. She reminded herself that there was no point dwelling on the past unpleasantness between her family and this man. Not when the new unpleasantness between the Banners and the Hollisters needed their immediate attention. Her fingers fell away from her collar. Odd how she'd never noticed before how snugly it rode against her throat. She squared her shoulders, determined to permanently banish the hostility between their two families before it tainted the next generation of Hollisters and Banners.

Grace cleared her throat, inwardly prepared to do battle—er, calmly and rationally discuss the situation between their ten-year-old sons. To be exact, two fiercely loyal warring sons.

"Mr. Hollister?" she inquired, pleased by her smooth professional tone.

There was a slight shifting of the leather work boots, then silence. She repeated her question louder. From beneath the station wagon came an ominous clang of metal, several pings and then a low gurgling sound. A deep, masculine voice swore. Pithily.

The mechanic's creeper supporting the long-legged body came shooting out from beneath the station wagon, and she jumped from its path. The top half of Matthew Hollister rolled into view—shirtless.

As he got to his feet, Grace's soft lips formed an unconscious, silent Oh. And, for a moment her eyes were too filled with chest to notice the turbulent, dark eyes staring down at her from an oil-splattered face.

Matthew Hollister reached past her to grab a fistful of paper towels from a nearby dispenser. "Can't you read?" he demanded impatiently, obviously referring to the sign at the shop's entrance.

Before she could reply, his face disappeared into the handful of blue paper towels. Grace's gaze fell again to the naked torso filling her field of vision. It had been a long time since she'd been this close to a bare-chested man. Six years to be exact. She swallowed. Somehow in girding up her courage to meet face-to-face with Blake's longtime nemesis, she had not envisioned confronting him quite this way.

"Well, if you can't read, can you at least speak?" drawled the husky voice.

Her wide-eyed gaze shot upward and she felt a warmth that had nothing to do with the unseasonably hot October afternoon creep into her cheeks. From the neutral expression marking his oil-smudged face, Grace realized he probably didn't recognize her as Blake's widow. That realization gave her the feeling of having been granted a temporary reprieve. She didn't even want to think about his reaction when he discovered who she was and why she had tracked him down.

"Matthew Hollister," she began, firmly anchoring her thoughts on the worrisome business that had put her on this man's trail.

He nodded, his dark stare casually studying over her high-necked, white crepe blouse tucked neatly into a pencil-slim gray skirt. Though his gaze lingered at predictable locations, there was nothing insulting or suggestive about his perusal. His was just the traditional male investigation of an unfamiliar female in his territory.

Grace wished he weren't quite so tall, though. Surely the Creator could have stopped a couple of inches short on Matthew Hollister and still left him with imposing height.

The force of Matthew's gaze was tangible enough to make Grace want to erect a barrier of formality between them. She retreated a step and extended her right hand for a brisk, businesslike handshake, determined to squelch the tremors of uneasiness she could feel ricocheting through her.

Let the chips fall where they may. It wasn't exactly

a credo of hers, but there were times when extraordinary circumstances called for extra measures of courage.

"I'm the principal of Peninsula Elementary and—" Before Grace could continue, her gaze was jerked downward to where her hand had been absorbed into the moist heat of his oily grip.

"Oh...." For some reason, the sight of her slight hand overwhelmed by Matthew Hollister's powerful, faintly soiled one made her breath quicken.

"Well, Principal Lady," he drawled huskily. "I seem to have gotten you dirty."

He reached past her again, extracted several more paper towels from the wall dispenser and handed them to her.

"There's a sign at the shop's entrance that says, Employees Only. Didn't you see it?" he inquired good-naturedly, his initial impatience apparently gone.

She looked up, surprised by the half smile softening his rugged features. She somehow couldn't resist returning it. "I saw the sign, Mr. Hollister."

"And?"

She sighed. "And, since you haven't had the courtesy to return any of my phone calls or acknowledge the letter I sent you, I decided not to let a dusty scrap of cardboard prevent me from having this discussion with you."

Matthew Hollister's smile disappeared. "You've got my attention now. Why don't you tell me what this is about? Brian, I presume?"

Grace's smile also faded. Under the circumstances, she decided she could overlook Matthew Hollister's faintly pugnacious expression. But she couldn't shut out the unsettling reality of his broad, softly furred chest. "Do you have a shirt, Mr. Hollister?"

"I make it a point never to leave home without one," he growled softly, then turned and presented her with a panorama of tautly sculptured back muscles. He stretched a long arm toward the denim work shirt that hung on a nearby nail.

"You'll have to excuse my manners." He shrugged the shirt over powerful shoulders and turned to face her, his fingers absently fastening its metallic buttons. He finished three short of the top.

She was tempted to suggest he keep on buttoning, but decided not to press the issue. At least with a shirt on, Matthew Hollister no longer seemed quite so frankly...naked.

At Grace's tentative smile, Matthew's features softened. He found himself wanting to accommodate her sense of modesty. Moments before he'd felt grubby and out of sorts, but as he stared into the stranger's lovely face, his mood lightened considerably. It certainly wasn't her fault that the inside of the shop was like a furnace, and he wasn't the hotshot mechanic he'd remembered himself being.

When Matthew had agreed to help his dad out of a bind and fill in at the garage, he'd looked at it as an opportunity to take a side trip down memory lane and revisit a period in his life when working with his hands had been his life. He flexed his right hand, staring at the skinned knuckles. Next time he saw a kid with a scraped knee, he was going to be a whole lot more sympathetic.

A couple of hours before the lady principal's arrival, he'd already admitted to himself that the reality of rusted-on bolts, failing air conditioners and stiff joints had considerably dulled nostalgia's appeal. This favor for his dad was accomplishing some good, however. He was spending a lot more time with his son.

Matthew took a moment to size up the primly dressed woman who was looking everywhere but directly at him. She was indeed very lovely, but obviously not his type. Not of course that he was attracted to a particular type of woman. He just knew instinctively that this one would be uncomfortable in the rough-and-tumble world of a blue-collar worker. He conveniently ignored the fact that, until a few weeks ago, his world had consisted of presiding over a multimillion-dollar chain of auto-repair franchises. And would so again in the near future.

"Why don't you tell me about these mysterious messages you claim to have left for me?" he suggested quietly.

Under Matthew Hollister's steady gaze, Grace felt strangely short of breath, as if she'd just sprinted the last ten yards of the Banner's Point annual Fourth of July marathon. "I've tried to reach you by telephone, I've mailed a letter requesting a conference, Mr. Hollister, and—"

He interrupted her. "What address did you send it to? My son and I moved to Banner's Point in August.

We were staying at my parents' home until a couple of weeks ago. Maybe the post office didn't know where to forward it.''

As far as Grace was concerned, no single statement from Matthew Hollister could have more clearly emphasized his being alien to the community. Estelle Milo had ruled Banner's Point's tiny cinder-block post office for so many years that no letter routed through her domain ever went undelivered through lack of a forwarding address. Grace had discovered that minor miracle six years ago when she'd moved from Virginia to Idaho.

Then a new thought struck Grace. If he'd forgotten the formidable Estelle Milo during his years away from the Point, what else had Matthew Hollister forgotten? It was obvious from the lack of hostility in his dark eyes that he hadn't yet placed her as Blake's widow. A twinge of irritation blunted Grace's earlier relief that her husband's former rival hadn't recognized her—irritation at being forgotten when she would have recognized him anywhere, under any circumstances.

''Then the letter would have been returned to me,'' Grace pointed out evenly.

''Brian usually picks up the mail. When I get home, I'll ask him if he knows anything about this missing letter. In the meantime, why don't you tell me what my son's been up to?''

Grace appreciated the man's no-nonsense directness. She decided to be just as direct. ''Brian is having difficulty adapting to our school. Something has to be done before his behavior gets out of hand.''

''I hadn't realized Brian was having problems. He's always been a good student.''

''I know; his transfer records show he received above average grades at his former school. That's why I'm so concerned.''

''It's only the first of October. Maybe he just needs more time to adjust to our move.'' Matthew's somber expression radiated concern for his son.

''I believe Brian's mother is—'' Grace paused, reluctant to broach so sensitive a subject with a virtual stranger.

''Brian's mother is dead,'' he finished quietly.

''That's what I understood.'' Grace could feel her initial hostility toward him fading. Surely between the two of them they could improve their sons' attitudes toward each other. ''I'm here today to see how we can help Brian be the same kind of student at Peninsula Elementary he was at his Los Angeles school. We need to figure out how to help him cope with a new school, new friends and a new neighborhood.''

Matthew eyed the large, round clock above the pop machine. ''It's after five, and I've had as much of this saltbox as I can take. My parents live down the street. Let me lock up, and we can go there to discuss this.''

Matthew Hollister's parents' home was a modest but comfortable brick house off the Peninsula's main street. Grace couldn't help but contrast the neat living room decorated in beiges and blues with Blake's parents' impressive home. The Banners' three-story, pillared, multigabled residence could qualify as an honest-to-goodness mansion.

Grace and her son, Jason, could have shared the house with Blake's parents. But she had summoned all the quiet persistence she could muster to stake a claim for independence. She and Jason lived in a home very similar to the one in which she now found herself.

Matthew Hollister excused himself to wash up, and the subsequent sounds of a shower in use testified to his thoroughness.

Grace leaned back against the tweed sofa's comfortable cushions and closed her eyes. Unexpectedly the stirring image of Matthew Hollister showering leaped into her tired mind. Unfortunately for her pulse rate, he wasn't performing the act fully clothed. Her gray eyes sprang open. Good grief, what was wrong with her? She wasn't some giddy adolescent whose thoughts gravitated toward virile, muscle-bound hunks. Of course, to be fair, Matthew Hollister wasn't muscle-bound. No, his was the sleek, well-toned physique of a basketball player.

When Grace realized she was now imagining the man dressed in, of all things, slinky, skimpy basketball trunks, she frowned and shifted her position on the sofa. There was no doubt about it. This new school year was proving to be a real challenge. Absently she massaged her temples, trying to lessen the familiar throbbing pressure that was beginning to build. Another headache, she thought dispiritedly. She knew the culprit was the workmen's endless hammering as they erected Peninsula's new elementary school.

Letting her thoughts drift for a few moments, Grace remembered how ecstatic she'd been when the three-million-dollar school bond had passed last spring. Banner's Point desperately needed a new elementary school. The original building had been erected in 1938. And even though the two-story brick structure had been kept in superior condition by its caretakers, a new school had been urgently needed to alleviate the overcrowding in the classrooms.

Grace was sure the impossible conditions in the fifth grade were the reason Brian Hollister was having so much difficulty adjusting to his move to Banner's Point. That and the fact that he had to share the same classroom with her son, Jason.

The school board had discussed splitting the class and having morning and afternoon sessions for the fifth-graders, as they did with the kindergarten children. But there simply weren't enough school buses in the district to shuttle another group of elementary students twice a day.

And little Brian Hollister and the rest of the fifth grade at Peninsula Elementary were victims of the intolerable situation. Grace's thoughts went to Jason, and her brows contracted in frustration.

It was a shame the two boys had decided to become mortal enemies, catching their teacher, Miss Hopkins, her two assistants and the entire fifth grade in the cross fire of their antagonism. And Blake's parents certainly hadn't helped the situation by resurrecting the fevered rhetoric of the long-ago campaign their son had successfully waged against Matthew Hollister. Why couldn't they let bygones be bygones?

Just a few minutes in Matthew Hollister's presence had shown her that the past could be buried. Matthew Hollister had forgotten it. He hadn't even remembered what she looked like. Ten years after the election was more than long enough to let the notorious Hollister/ Banner competition end. Especially when Blake was dead.

Matthew Hollister's quiet voice broke into Grace's troubled thoughts. "Sorry I took so long."

He strode into the room wearing a pale blue shirt with the cuffs rolled back to expose tanned forearms dusted with dark hair. Gray dress slacks outlined his long, muscular legs, emphasizing his lean, fit physique. Tiny droplets of water shimmered in his neatly combed dark hair. And Grace found herself gazing into a strong face devoid of its earlier smudges of oil.

Matthew Hollister was…more. More than she had remembered. He was not a conventionally handsome man, however. His features were far too uneven for so kind a label. Three lines creased his forehead, and his cheekbones were sharply defined, as were his nose and aggressive jaw. The dark eyes that held her in their grip were too direct, too probing to be described by any word as tame as *handsome*. No, she would never call Matthew Hollister handsome, but he *was* rugged and virile and…unforgettable. An uncompromisingly masculine man.

"Do I pass inspection?" The subtle warmth in his voice and the faint gleam in his dark eyes hinted at his awareness that she was reacting to him on a physical level.

Grace watched him cross the room toward her. "You look cool and refreshed," she murmured noncommittally.

"I do? Funny, I'm feeling kind of warm and bothered, Principal Lady." There was a husky invitation in his deep voice. Not a come-on, just a straightforward acknowledgment that he was a man and she was a woman. And he found her to his liking.

Confused by Matthew Hollister's potent effect on her, Grace resolved once and for all to banish the heady crosscurrents of sensual awareness that seemed to be flowing beneath the civilized veneer of their conversation. Think Peninsula Elementary, she commanded herself.

"Actually, it's *Mrs.* Banner, and I've never known it to be so hot in Idaho during October."

The minute the words were out of her mouth, she wanted to call them back. The change in Matthew Hollister's expression was dramatic as his gaze zeroed in on the ring finger of her left hand. As he stared at her ornate engagement and wedding rings, a veil seemed to drop over his eyes, erecting an almost tangible barrier between them. And even though Grace had wished for that barrier, she now regretted its presence.

He moved across the room to a high-backed chair that faced the couch where she was sitting. "The weathermen are calling it a reprieve from our usual fall weather.''

"Knowing Idaho, I'd say we'll probably have snow on the ground by next weekend." Good grief, we're talking about the weather, Grace realized. With consternation she also realized Matthew Hollister still hadn't identified her as Blake's widow. Of course, the Peninsula boasted several families named Banner. But still—

"About my son, Mrs. Banner, what seems to be the problem?"

"Brian is a bright, energetic young man, Mr. Hollister," Grace began gently, wanting to soften her forthcoming complaints about the adorable demon. "Unfortunately he seems unwilling or unable to accept any discipline from his teacher, Miss Hopkins."

She paused, waiting for Matthew Hollister to jump in with a rebuttal on his son's behalf. Usually at this point in a conference, parents were defending their children's behavior. But Brian's father sat pensively across the room, waiting for her to continue.

"First of all, I think you have a right to know what kind of teacher Miss Hopkins is. She's a warm, dedicated woman, brimming with enthusiasm. We feel lucky to have her at Peninsula Elementary. She's been teaching for four years and usually has an excellent rapport with her students."

"Why didn't she contact me? Isn't that the usual procedure in a case like this?"

"Ordinarily she would have been the one to have this discussion with you, Mr. Hollister. But this is anything but an 'ordinary' year for us at Peninsula. I'm sure you've been by our school and have seen the construction in progress.''

"I have. That's quite a new schoolhouse you have going up.''

Grace flushed with pride. She couldn't help it. The new building with its equipment and teaching aids meant a lot to her. They'd all worked so hard to get the bond passed.

"Then I'm sure you've noticed the school is being built in the middle of what used to be Peninsula's playground. We plan to tear down the old school when the new one is finished, and then our playground will be there.''

"Good plan.''

"Yes, it was a good plan. On paper. But you can't imagine the kind of chaos you get with 675 school children at recess—with *no* playground.''

Matthew Hollister leaned forward in his chair and nodded sympathetically. "I can see where that might cause major pandemonium.''

"We moved a few of the bigger pieces of playground equipment onto the school's front lawn—some swings, monkey bars and a slide. But there's simply not enough room or equipment to go around.''

"What about the vacant lot across the street? It's about the size of a small park. Couldn't you set up additional playground equipment there?''

Grace smiled wistfully. "I had the same idea. I even approached the man who owns it to see if he'd let us use it, but he's trying to sell the lot. And he's afraid letting the elementary school use it will hurt his chances.''

''Doesn't seem likely.''

''With Randolph P. Henshaw, 'likely' doesn't enter into it. He just didn't want to be bothered.'' Grace's fingers went to her temples, and she massaged them to lessen the throbbing pressure.

''Would you like a couple of aspirin?''

She looked up, surprised by his perceptiveness in noticing she had a headache. ''Yes, thank you.''

Matthew stood and left the room. Moments later he returned with a tumbler in one hand and two aspirins in the other.

After swallowing the pills and drinking all the water, she returned the empty glass to him and rested her head against the back of the couch. ''Thank you. You can't imagine what it's like with that hammering going on all day. It's hard on the faculty and the students.''

''When's the new school going to be finished?'' He sat the empty glass on a nearby end table and joined her on the couch.

''The outside construction is supposed to be completed in three months. But we won't be able to use the new building until next fall.'' Matthew Hollister's proximity made Grace aware her skirt had ridden above her knees, and she discreetly tugged her hemline downward.

''Are any of the other kids having the problems Brian is?''

Grace sat up straight. She couldn't believe how

she'd strayed from the subject of Mr. Hollister's son. For a few moments all she'd thought about was how good it felt to talk with a sympathetic adult.

"There have been more discipline problems than usual this year. But Brian's behavior is not typical. In answer to your earlier question the reason I'm following through with this conference instead of Miss Hopkins is because she has fifty-four students in her class and—"

"What?" Matthew's air of quiet support vanished. "Fifty-four kids crammed into one classroom? You've got to be kidding. There's no way anyone could learn under those conditions."

"They meet in the gymnasium—"

He interrupted her. "With *one* teacher? I don't care if this Miss Hopkins is the greatest person alive; there's no way she can handle fifty-four ten-year-olds."

"She has two teaching assistants," Grace said, defensively. "But you're right. The situation is intolerable. We're doing the best we can, though, and I'm playing a very active part this year with the fifth grade. I make a point of spending almost two class periods daily in the gym. I'm also helping Miss Hopkins by assuming some of her parent-teacher duties."

"Lord, this must be one hell of a year for you." Matthew's dark eyes showed his concern for her plight.

She swallowed back the lump in her throat. It *had* been a hellish year. Lately she'd found herself wondering how she was going to survive it. She was putting in twelve-hour workdays, trying to keep up with housework and fighting for time to spend with Jason. She blinked back sudden, unexpected tears.

"I'm managing," she said with quiet strength. "But there are days…"

"I can imagine." As Matthew studied the delicate woman sitting next to him, he found himself wondering what *Mr.* Banner was doing to make his wife's burden easier to bear.

Now that he looked closer, he noticed Grace Banner was a little on the thin side. Oh, she had curves in all the right places—along with a damned fine pair of legs. But there was a hollowness to her high cheekbones and the beginnings of mauve smudges under those incredible gray eyes of hers, mute testimony to how hard she was pushing herself. Her rich, short mane of chestnut hair made her flawless complexion seem unnaturally pale.

Matthew Hollister's hands closed into fists as he restrained the surprising urge to draw Peninsula Elementary School's *married* principal into his arms. He scowled. He had already decided she wasn't the kind of woman to whom he should feel attracted.

Matthew straightened. A memory nudged him. Banner. It was a common-enough name, especially on the Point. But the softly appealing woman seated next to him was in no way common. She was one of a kind.

Matthew sucked in his breath. He knew her. Remembered her, anyway. She was of that dark and desperate time in his life. That time when, locked in a fierce political contest against his childhood nemesis, he had learned Cathy was dying of leukemia. The pain that shot through him was as real and sharp as the first time he'd felt it, when he'd learned his beloved Cathy might not live to bear their first child.

"The main problem with Brian seems to be a feud he's begun with another fifth-grader."

Matthew called on the herculean inner strength that had brought him through the darkest period of his life. "Would I sound too much like a biased parent if I asked how you know it was Brian who started the feud?"

Grace smiled. Uneasily. "Ah, well, yes.... The matter of bias does enter into the problem, Mr. Hollister."

He picked up on her nervousness immediately. "Why do I have the feeling I've just heard one shoe drop?"

"Because you've excellent hearing," Grace said with a sigh, looking up and meeting the dark eyes studying her so intently. "The boy your son has taken a royal dislike to is another bright and energetic young man—my son, Jason."

Matthew Hollister whistled softly. "I see." And he did. It was history repeating itself. How ironic that he'd only thought of the benefits of moving Brian to the Point, never once considering that the past might catch up with them. A past marked by his adolescent ambition to prove himself Blake Banner's equal in all things.

Grace had braced herself for an antagonistic response. Instead, she found herself looking into Matthew Hollister's thoughtful features.

"You're right, of course," she observed softly. "Brian and Jason are equally responsible for the trouble between them."

"So your son and my son don't like each other," he mused huskily, allowing his gaze to linger on her upturned face. "Strange. I like you, Grace Banner. It is Grace, isn't it?"

He had remembered her! When? she wondered, losing herself in the silent depths of his steady stare.

Before Grace could respond to his question, the front door banged open, and a piping young voice filled the room.

"Dad! Dad, you in here?" Thudding sneakers sounded on the carpeted floor. Then unruly dark hair, wide brown eyes, freckles and an all-American, boyish grin that could melt the sternest heart flashed into view.

Grace had difficulty controlling a smile at Brian's crestfallen expression when he realized who was sitting on the couch talking to his father. The ten-year-old skidded to a halt a couple of feet in front of the sofa.

"Hi, Dad," he drawled at last with a commendable attempt at nonchalance.

"Hi, son," his father replied dryly.

Grace bit her bottom lip to suppress a highly unprofessional chuckle. The Hollister men were probably natural-born poker players. Neither of them acted as if there was anything amiss in Brian's principal paying them a visit.

"Aren't you going to say hello to Mrs. Banner?" Matthew Hollister asked casually, his dark eyes sparkling with affectionate humor.

Grace sensed the warmhearted love father and son shared. So this was the loving, teasing camaraderie a man shared with his children. The memory of her own father flashed into Grace's mind. As a businessman, he had been a spectacular success. But as a parent he'd been emotionally inaccessible.

And before her husband's untimely death, the incredible demands of political office had robbed him of the time necessary to build a nurturing relationship with their son. Thus, both she and Jason had been denied the kind of close masculine intimacy Matthew Hollister obviously shared with Brian.

"Hello, Mrs. Banner," mumbled the boy.

"Hello, Brian. Your father and I have been having a little chat."

"It seems that a letter Mrs. Banner mailed to me has gone astray," Matthew Hollister said quietly. "Do you want to tell me about it, son?"

Grace rose to her feet, and Brian eyed her uneasily. "Perhaps it would be a good idea for you and Brian to talk about this privately first," she suggested, moving toward the front door. "I'll have my secretary call you to schedule a conference at school."

Matthew also stood, fighting the sudden temptation to reach out and unfasten the top pearl button of Grace Banner's silk blouse. He found himself wanting to do *something* to ruffle her entirely proper demeanor. Wisely he chose instead to withdraw his wallet from his back pocket and extract a business card.

"I'll give you our new phone number." He jotted the number on the back of the card and extended it to her.

Grace reached out, strangely conscious of the stark contrast of his bruised, tanned hand against her pale white one. She glanced briefly at the card and noticed it sported the Divine Deliverance logo—a gleaming vintage convertible.

Matthew opened the front door and then followed her outside. "I'm glad you tracked me down today. I care about my son, and I wouldn't have wanted something like this to drag on without me knowing about it. Thank you, Grace."

Standing on the front steps, Grace stared into his serious face. Dark eyes filled with integrity and strength gazed down at her, holding her with their intensity. Dusk had fallen, and a ribbon of coolness snaked through the unseasonably warm night air. She shivered.

"How long did it take you to realize who I was?" she asked softly.

Chapter Two

Matthew studied her pale features. "Longer than it should have. I was noticing how tired you looked and wondered what your husband was doing to help you. I looked at you and thought of Blake."

"Are Blake Banner's son and Matthew Hollister's son going to follow in their fathers' footsteps and be enemies?" The question had not been planned, but Grace was very curious to hear his response.

"Blake and I never were enemies, only rivals."

"Our sons don't seem able to tell the difference."

"If you're right, we've got a major problem on our hands, Principal Lady."

Grace nodded, fascinated by how, in the ripening twilight, Matthew Hollister's eyes seemed to deepen to an impossible shade of midnight black. Shaking her head in bemusement, she muttered a hasty goodbye.

The blocks to her modest home passed in a quiet

daze. Dusk mantled the lonely sidewalks of Banner's Point. And in the houses she passed, the lights were turned on to blunt the coming night. Grace realized it was suppertime and quickened her pace. She needed to get home to Jason.

Despite the briskness of her steps, Matthew Hollister's parting words lingered in her mind. She told herself it was the cooling evening air and not the deep pitch of his husky voice that had caused her flesh to tingle.

Later that night as Grace methodically loaded the dinner plates into the dishwasher, she was still trying to come to terms with her physical reaction to Matthew Hollister. Taking an absent swipe with a damp dishrag at the blue tile countertop, she wrinkled her nose.

Obviously her heavy work schedule was taking a toll on her. It was inconceivable that she could feel any sensual attraction to a man who'd once been Blake's enemy.

No, not enemy. Matthew had set her straight on that point. But Blake and Matthew had once been fierce political opponents. And thus it followed that... That what? That she would feel nothing but animosity toward Matthew Hollister? Somehow animosity didn't begin to describe her ambivalent feelings for the compelling man.

Feeling strangely confused, Grace tried to understand why meeting Matthew Hollister had affected her so strongly. He was just a man, after all.

In the six years since Blake's death, she'd dated

several people. At first she'd felt awkward and unsure of herself. Gradually those feelings had passed, and now hardly a month went by without her enjoying a casual outing with one of her male friends. But none of those friends had entered her life with the impact of Matthew Hollister. She certainly had never imagined any of them in a pair of orange satin basketball trunks! Or in a shower, either.

Grace gave the compact kitchen a final glance. It was a far cry from the palatial cooking center her home in Arlington had boasted. And yet, she didn't regret for a moment her decision to sell the colonial-style house she and Blake had owned in Virginia to settle in southern Idaho where she and Jason could be close to Blake's parents. But not so close that they shared the same house.

She had always gotten along well with her in-laws, so the decision to relocate in Idaho hadn't been a difficult one. Her own mother had died just before Jason was born and her father had remarried eight years ago. He had a new family now. One that seemed to satisfy him more than his old one had.

The situation only bothered Grace to the extent that it affected Jason. She'd come to terms years ago with the knowledge she and her father would never be close. She was just glad he'd found someone to share his life with. It would disturb her if she thought he was lonely. No one should be alone. Before flicking off the kitchen light, she bowed her head and said a silent prayer of gratitude that she had Jason. It was the two of them against the world.

Jason. He had thrived in the small community of Banner's Point, and she felt a major portion of his happiness there was due to Blake's parents' unapologetic doting on him. But there was no getting around the fact that these two wonderful people were the same grandparents who had loudly bemoaned Matthew Hollister's return. Of course she'd been disturbed, too, when she'd first heard he was moving back to the Point.

But after talking to him, she realized he harbored no ill feelings toward the Banners. Between the two of them, they'd surely be able to get their sons to feel the same way.

When she entered her family room, Grace's gaze went directly to her son. Jason shared the comfortable, caramel-colored sofa with a load of laundry still warm from the dryer. Engrossed in a fast-paced crime drama she loathed, he hardly seemed to blink as the scenes of blazing guns and exploding cars flickered across the screen. Friday night and *L.A. Cops*. It was almost more than a sane person could bear.

Before Grace's nerves could snap at the unrestrained carnage, relief in the form of a Divine Deliverance commercial appeared. She paused for moment to watch. This particular ad was one of her favorites. A teenage boy nervously asked his dad if he could borrow the family car for his first date. The boy, wearing blue jeans and a tattered T-shirt, walked out to an old clunker of a car parked in front of his home, then drove into a Divine Deliverance dealership. In the last scene, the beaming boy picked up his date wearing a suit and tie. His hair was neatly slicked down, and the car had been beautifully restored.

Divine Deliverance or D.D., as it was commonly referred to, was a national chain of auto-repair franchises specializing in refurbishing older automobiles.

It was a multimillion-dollar company, and Matthew Hollister had built it from nothing more than a simple idea and hard work. He was the owner and president of the corporation. And to the citizens of Banner's Point, he was proof positive that even today it was possible to start from scratch and achieve the American dream.

Then another commercial came on, and Jason's attention wavered. "Mom, you're coming to the soccer game tomorrow, aren't you? It's our last one this year."

"Wouldn't miss it for the world, honey." She briskly shook the faint creases from a lemon-colored pillowcase before folding it into a neat square. "Ten a.m. at the park, right?"

"Right. We're playing the Rigby Rustlers. It's going to be awesome."

"Sounds like it." She reached for another pillowcase. Then, sensing her son's solemn stare, she looked up. "Is something wrong?"

"The guys at school think you're pretty," he said in a rush.

"Really?" She smiled at the thought of having a flock of miniature admirers.

"I think so, too. I'd rather have a mom like you

than a dad like Brian Hollister's any day of the week,'' he added emphatically.

Grace felt the muscles in her throat tighten. Poor Jason. It was natural for him to want a father. Mixed up with his feelings of hostility toward Brian Hollister was probably a healthy measure of jealousy. Brian had a dad. Jason didn't. It didn't take a degree in psychology to realize that such feelings of jealousy would make Jason feel guilty. Envying Brian because of Matthew would surely seem like a kind of betrayal to Jason's own father.

Grace blinked back unexpected tears, tears she didn't feel she should shed in front of her son. She had to be strong for both of them. That was the legacy Blake's death had left in her life.

''I'm 'awesome,' hmm?'' Her voice quavered only a little bit.

''Yeah, awesome,'' concurred Jason, his attention pulled back to the television by the sound of squealing brakes. ''Brian Hollister called you a fox.''

''A fox,'' she repeated in surprise.

''That's California talk for pretty.''

''Thanks for the translation.'' Her eyes glistened with unshed tears and tenderness. Lord, how she loved Jason.

Trying to ignore the three drug dealers being gunned to death in her living room, she decided to shift the subject to Brian. ''Are you and he getting along any better?''

''Who?''

She sighed at her son's deliberate obtuseness. "Brian."

"We're getting along just fine," Jason mumbled.

Grace decided to let the matter drop. She had made it a policy to keep school business at school. If Jason had done something to further annoy Brian Hollister, she would take it up with him Monday morning.

She glanced down at the comfortable pair of jeans and the pale pink T-shirt she'd changed into before fixing dinner and couldn't help smiling. So some of Jason's friends thought she was pretty. Funny, in the past few years her role as a working mother had consumed so much of her time and thoughts, she hadn't really considered her looks that much.

Before she'd moved to Banner's Point, she hadn't even owned a pair of jeans. But somehow, being the mother of a rambunctious four-year-old who had loved to roughhouse had gotten her out of silk and into denim in a hurry.

As her gaze rested on Jason's thick honey-colored hair and green eyes, her smile turned reflective. A younger version of Blake, he was at the point in his life where there was very little left of the chubby toddler he'd once been and a strong element of the man he would one day become. He really wasn't a little boy anymore.

Their six years on the Peninsula had changed her, too. She'd become more self-sufficient and self-confident, stronger emotionally than when Blake had been alive. She supposed his death had forced her to dig inside herself to find the layer of bedrock stamina a woman needed to raise a child alone. Her gaze drifted back to her son. Her love for him and her demanding job as principal had become her entire world.

The Peninsula Pirates scored a hard-earned field goal against the Rigby Rustlers, and Grace, along with the other parents in the stands, cheered enthusiastically. "Way to go!"

Her gaze lingered briefly on the sidelines and she caught sight of Brian Hollister's crop of unruly dark hair. Next to him stood his father. Dressed in a maroon cable-knit sweater and well-worn blue jeans that molded his long, powerful legs, Matthew Hollister looked... The word that popped into her mind was *delicious*, but she squashed it.

While she watched Matthew address the Pirates' coach, Edgar Potter, Grace chided herself for her improper thoughts. She couldn't imagine where the naughty little demons were coming from. She simply wasn't the kind of woman who...who lusted after men. Ever. Well, hardly ever. Not real flesh-and-blood ones, anyway.

She shifted on the hard wooden bench. Her occasional fantasies were generally reserved for those swashbuckling heroes found in historical romances. The kind of men who were tough and hard and driven by noble quests until they were bewitched by virtuous young maidens. Young maidens whose innocent blood flowed with surprising heat. Grace frowned softly. Perhaps it was time she expanded her reading to include more realistic plots. The realities of present-day life afforded precious little space for old-time heroes. Her frown faded, and the corners of her mouth curved upward. Oh, but those heroes did make splendid pirates.

Grace decided she'd better concentrate on what was happening on the playing field. Coach Potter had signaled for a time-out and was motioning for Jason to leave the game. Uh-oh, he was putting Brian Hollister in to play Jason's position.

Grace gritted her teeth in frustration. It wasn't that she minded Jason being taken out. She sincerely believed every boy should have a chance to play. But she would have preferred Jason to be replaced by *anyone* other than Brian Hollister. There were few things in life Jason took as seriously as his soccer. This development did not bode well for a lull in the continuing war between the two boys.

From Jason's jerky movements as he walked off the soccer field, Grace's troubled gaze shifted to Matthew Hollister. He must have sensed her stare, for his dark head turned from the field to scan the stands. Mere seconds passed before he caught sight of her.

He moved forward, his long legs swiftly bringing him to where she was seated. "Hello, Grace."

The sound of her name emerging from his firm lips brought a flush to her cheeks.

"Good morning, Matthew." It felt strange using his first name, but pleasant. Disconcertingly so.

In the morning sunlight, his lean face reflected good health and a masculine vitality that made her heartbeat quicken. When he sat down next to her, Grace scooted over to give him room. Even so, the solid, muscular length of his leg brushed against her slacks. Through the durable material she could feel her thigh tremble.

"I assume one of those tireless young men is your son. Which one is he?"

At the sound of his deep voice vibrating in her ear, Grace jumped. It took a moment for her to frame a neutral reply. "The golden-haired boy Brian just replaced."

Matthew turned to her with a chagrined expression. "Uh-oh."

"My sentiments exactly. Not that I mind Jason sitting out for a few minutes," she added hastily.

"It's just that your boy now has one more grievance to hold against mine, right?"

Grace nodded.

"We've got major trouble all right," he muttered grimly, directing his gaze back to the game.

As they watched the boys, Grace became aware of a multitude of sensations. In the distance, mountains ringed the plains surrounding them, the snowy peaks hinting at the coming winter. And yet, overriding that vague impression was the summerlike heat emanating from Matthew's body. The soft caress of the October sun on her face seemed to balance between the two opposing seasons.

But crowding out the other impressions was Grace's uncanny feeling that she'd survived a violent winter storm and had at last reached a safe, warm harbor. They were foolish, disquieting feelings, but poignant ones, ones impossible to banish. And she knew that somehow they were linked to the man, sitting beside her.

"Your son knows his way around a soccer field," Grace observed softly, watching Brian zigzag through three Rigby Rustlers.

"If your son's anything like his father, he's a dynamite athlete himself." Matthew sensed Grace's tension at his reference to Blake.

He had no desire to cause her distress, but in the past few weeks he'd made the disheartening discovery that the citizens of Banner's Point had kept alive the legend of his rivalry with Blake Banner.

Damn. It almost seemed that their long-ago competition was more notorious today than it had been when he and Blake were growing up. He sliced a glance at Blake's widow and grinned, despite his pensive mood. His old rival had done pretty well for himself in choosing a wife. Grace Banner was a class act. The grin deepened. Her neatly pressed, brushed-denim slacks and long-sleeved pink blouse were similar to the casual outfits the other mothers in the stands wore. But on Grace Banner the combination went together in a stylish way that could have carried her through a tea party with the First Lady.

Idly he wondered if she had ever tasted a beer. Somehow he couldn't visualize her dainty, pink tongue taking a delicate swipe at a foamy upper lip. His grin died. He had no business thinking about her pink tongue—dainty or otherwise—in any context.

This woman had belonged to Blake. She could never mean anything to him. That was one rule that, even though he'd made it years ago when he and Blake had courted the same fresh-faced cheerleader, he never intended breaking.

Linda. The girl's name had been Linda. She'd been dating Blake a couple of months and, because of a stupid bet, he'd decided to get her to accept a date with him. Only things had gotten out of hand and the situation had escalated on Linda's side. And he'd had to live with the guilt of knowing that the girl's main attraction for him had been her involvement with Blake.

He clenched his hands into tight fists. It wasn't an episode he could remember without a flush of shame. Afterward, when he'd sorted out his feelings, he had to accept the fact that the competitiveness between himself and Blake had seeped into other areas of their lives. It was then he'd decided any girl who dated Blake was taboo. And since Linda, he'd honored that taboo. No woman intimately involved with Blake had a place in his life. Deliberately he relaxed his tensed hand muscles. As for Blake's widow, she was absolutely off limits.

Grace's prolonged silence began to grate on Matthew's nerves. When he'd referred to her husband, he hadn't meant to offend her. "Does it bother you to talk about Blake?"

He studied her clean profile, fascinated while he watched a slight flush steal up her pale cheeks. He wished he'd thought before he'd spoken. He wouldn't have appreciated her inquiring about Cathy.

"Maybe a little—with you."

She turned, focusing her incredible gray eyes on him. He felt as if someone had jabbed him with a body punch aimed straight at his stomach. Needless to say, she had his undivided attention.

"I can understand that. Blake and I were never friends." He didn't add that he had respected the man and would have liked his friendship, that he'd often regretted the fact that circumstances had always seemed to put them in the same arena as competitors.

Grace recalled Blake's father's account of Blake and Matthew's youthful rivalry. The young men had tried out for high school varsity basketball, both vying to start as center. Blake had won that contest. But it was Matthew who'd won the battle for first-string quarterback on the varsity football squad. Blake had been shifted to start as a running back. Matthew had been captain of the team his junior and senior years.

It had been Blake, however, who'd come out the winner in the school election for student-body president—by six votes. The school campaign still ranked as the high school's closest election. And of course Blake had won the state election for Congress against Matthew. That contest had been almost as close as the one in high school. In the congressional contest, only a two-hundred-vote difference had made Blake the winner. No, she supposed Matthew and Blake hadn't exactly been friends.

"But Blake was never your enemy," Grace reaffirmed aloud.

"That's right." One side of Matthew's mouth tilted at the corner. "But there was a time or two when I considered him a real pain in the...neck."

She couldn't help smiling at the gentle irony in Matthew's deep voice or the friendly wink he gave her. A slight breeze had come up, ruffling his thick hair. She could almost imagine it was a woman's fingertips slipping through its dark, rich texture.

She swallowed, or at any rate tried to. Why was she so aware of his slightly parted, firm lips? Were they sitting closer than before? A tiny jolt of electricity seemed to leap between them, and Grace felt herself sway toward him, pulled by some invisible yet inexorable force beyond her control.

Then suddenly, the parents around them were on their feet, cheering for the Pirates. Instinctively Grace and Matthew stood, both jarred by the intense physical attraction they'd just experienced.

All around them, people were laughing and congratulating one another on another Pirate win. Numbly, Grace realized the game was over. She had no memory of even having watched the last part of it.

"Did you see me, Dad?" shouted Brian Hollister, leaping across the bleacher seats. "I scored the winning goal!"

A dull red flush crept up Matthew's neck, and Grace realized that he, too, had been preoccupied with matters other than junior-league soccer and had missed the last play of the game.

Matthew shot Grace a rueful grin, then turned to Brian. "Way to go, son!"

"Mom! You gonna stand there all day?" Jason demanded impatiently.

Her gaze went to her son. He stood at the bottom of the stands, looking disgusted with life in general and her in particular. His green eyes met hers reproachfully, and she had the feeling that Benedict Arnold had stood a better chance at getting a fair hearing from George Washington than she would from Jason. Clearly he saw her conversation with Matthew Hollister and his son as consorting with the enemy.

"Goodbye, Grace."

That voice. It seemed to speak to her on more than one level of awareness. She turned and faced Matthew.

"Goodbye." Her glance fell on Brian. "Congratulations, Brian. It looks like the Pirates have another super player on the team."

"Thank you, Mrs. Banner."

"Mom!" Jason's shout could have rivaled a lion's roar. A very irritated lion.

Gingerly stepping down the bleachers, Grace caught sight of Reverend Jensen. She hoped his sermon tomorrow would touch on loving one's neighbor. And forgiveness. That was always a good topic. Charity, tolerance and turning the other cheek were good subjects, too. And honoring one's father and mother carried a strong message. Eyeing Jason's ramrod-stiff posture, Grace wondered if the good reverend might possibly incorporate all six ideas into his sermon.

Chapter Three

"Dad, are you asleep?"

With a groan, Matthew rolled over onto his stomach.

"Dad." Small but determined hands shook his shoulder without particular gentleness.

One eyelid opened, revealing a glaring, bloodshot eyeball. "Brian, is that you?"

"Yeah, Dad. It's time to get up. We've only got an hour till church starts."

"Oh." His mind a bucket of cold mush, Matthew sat up slowly. He rubbed the back of his neck for a moment before swinging his legs to the floor. Then, both eyelids snapped open, revealing two glaring, bloodshot eyes.

"We don't go to church, Brian." He flopped back down on the bed.

Ordinarily Matthew didn't overindulge in alcohol,

but somehow at two in the morning, after he'd gotten off the marathon phone call with Doug Ryan, he'd felt like having more than a token toast to his problems. Oh, he still felt good about his selection of Doug Ryan to run D.D. in his absence. And he had full confidence in the man's ability to oversee the relocation of the corporate headquarters to Idaho Falls. But who could have guessed how many legal and technical complications would be involved in transplanting his business to a new town?

Matthew didn't delude himself that his drinking had been caused solely by Doug's call. He admitted to himself that he'd been missing Cathy. Well, perhaps not Cathy so much. It had been nine years since her death, after all. No, what he'd been missing was the sweet, loving comfort only a woman could provide. He'd been in the mood to hold and be held. He'd been in the mood for some rough-and-tumble loving. And the tenderness, too. In short, he'd been in the mood for a woman.

Somehow Grace Banner's image had crept into his thoughts—her lustrous crop of chestnut curls, big gray eyes and perfectly sculpted nose. He had recalled the soft, beckoning shape of her delicate mouth and her eminently touchable complexion. A woman most definitely. But not the woman for his dark bedroom fantasy. All prim and proper, she'd probably have an allergic reaction to anything as racy as black satin sheets. If she didn't faint first.

He knew he was being unfair to her. But alone in the quiet of the night, with only his hunger to keep him company, he hadn't wanted to be fair. After all, was it fair that he should feel such a strong physical and emotional tug toward a woman who was most definitely off-limits to him?

He had assured himself that his attraction to Grace was only a temporary aberration on his part and that he'd get over it. Grace had been Blake's. That said it all. She could have no place in his life.

And if she'd been any other man's widow?

Would he have felt the same attraction toward her? That had been the question he'd found no answer to. And it had been with that unanswerable thought ringing in his ears that Matthew Hollister had gotten quietly, stinkingly drunk.

Clearly feeling that he'd given his dad enough time to wake up, Brian declared his youthful convictions. "Dad, I think it's time we started going to church."

"Does it have to be *this* morning?" Matthew mumbled from beneath the pillow he'd just pulled over his head.

"I'm all ready, Dad."

The corner of the pillow raised an inch, and Matthew surveyed his son, noticing for the first time that the boy was impeccably dressed in a shirt and dress slacks. And he was squeaky clean. Matthew digested that last discovery.

"Uh, Brian, today isn't Easter or anything, is it?"

Brian laughed. "Come on, dad, you'll like it. Reverend Jensen is a real neat preacher."

"When did you meet Reverend Jensen?"

"At the game yesterday. They have a cub scout

den at the church, dad. I'd really like to join. I'd be a Webelo and learn all kinds of good stuff—tying ropes, and building fires and tracking wild animals.''

Matthew relinquished his death grip on the pillow and sat up again. ''Somehow I don't find those skills particularly desirable.''

''I heard they're looking for a new den leader, Dad.''

''What happened to the old one? Did he find one of those wild animals?''

''Naw. It was a lady, and she got pregnant.'' Brian made her fate sound worse than if she had met up with a man-eating tiger.

''Too bad.''

''You ever think of being a den leader, Dad?''

''Not lately.''

''Might be kinda of fun, don't you think?''

Matthew lunged to his feet and then grimaced. ''Come on, son. If we don't hurry, we're going to be late for church.''

''Yeah, right,'' said Brian glumly.

''And of course, I need to find out how someone goes about qualifying for den leader of the Wackalos.''

Brian laughed excitedly. ''It's Webelos.''

''Got it. Webelos.''

It was with some reluctance that Matthew Hollister came to the conclusion that Grace Banner dressed in a white wool suit and pale yellow silk blouse was the most softly appealing woman he'd ever seen sitting next to a stained-glass window. But then not many of the women he knew frequented churches.

He couldn't stop staring at her. She and her son were sitting in the pew just in front of him and Brian. Faint rays of color bathed her face and clothes. She looked like something sprung from the pages of a fairy tale. A young princess?

No, there was nothing girlish about Grace Banner. She might be shy and a little restrained for his taste, but she was every inch a woman. He noticed how her arm draped affectionately over her son's shoulders. He sensed that she was a conscientious mother. Had she been with another man since Blake's death? That errant thought rumbled through Matthew's composure with the impact of a giant-sized boulder careening down a mountainside. Whether the lady had or hadn't was none of his business. He stared at her more intently. He'd bet a bundle she hadn't.

It wasn't easy, but Matthew jerked his gaze from the lady in question and forced himself to concentrate on Reverend Jensen's sermon. He suspected a man might be held accountable for entertaining certain thoughts in a church.

"And thus, brothers and sisters, we must never forget that the Lord was with those hardy pioneers who crossed the American plains, heading west."

Oh, drat, thought Grace. One would think with a one-out-of-six chance, Reverend Jensen could have covered a subject closer to home. She glanced at Jason. He sat with sticklike stiffness beneath her arm. It was amazing that a boy so young could be so adroit in giving the cold shoulder. And he'd been even more sour-faced after his Sunday-school class. She really hoped this was just a phase he was going through—a very short one.

She glanced at the pew behind her. Evidently Matthew Hollister found the reverend's message more compelling than she did. His sharply defined features seemed locked in concentration on the minister's sermon. Dressed in a dark blue suit that contrasted starkly with his white shirt and burgundy tie, Matthew Hollister had to be the most ruggedly appealing man ever to attend services in this chapel.

"...blizzards, hostile Indians and disease. Yes, the pioneers endured all those privations and more."

Grace pulled her gaze away from Matthew Hollister and tried to give Reverend Jensen her full attention. It wasn't easy. Somehow she was fiercely aware of Matthew's closeness in the pew behind her. Was he going to join their congregation? This was the first time she'd seen him at church, and she and Jason attended services every Sunday. She told herself that Matthew Hollister's church attendance, the state of his eternal soul and how handsomely he filled out a suit had nothing to do with her.

After the service, Grace and her son moved through the clusters of churchgoers to the front of the chapel. As if fate had decreed it, she and Jason stepped through the entry and encountered the Hollisters on the steps.

The pastor was extending his hand to Matthew.

"Mr. Hollister, it's a pleasure to welcome you to our church."

"It's a pleasure to meet you, Reverend Jensen. When I was a boy, Vincent Holmes was the pastor here." He glanced at the white-frame edifice. "Other than that, everything else seems to have remained unchanged."

The reverend tipped his balding head to one side. "My sermons are a little different from my predecessor's."

Matthew grinned. "They're shorter."

Reverend Jensen chuckled. "I believe in getting to the point."

"I never realized just how many trials the pioneers had to overcome," returned Matthew, sincerely impressed by the reverend's account of their suffering.

"You may gain a first-hand knowledge of overcoming trials," suggested the reverend with a surprisingly wicked gleam in his normally innocent blue eyes. "I've heard you've volunteered to be the Webelos den leader."

"Oh, barf," protested Jason in a voice loud enough for Matthew to hear. Both Grace's and Matthew's faces pinkened, while Brian's hands clenched into tight fists.

"As I said, you've got your trials ahead of you, Mr. Hollister," repeated the reverend, turning his attention to Grace.

In record time, Grace thanked the pastor for his sermon and ushered Jason to their car. Blows hadn't been exchanged yet between the two boys, and she aimed to keep it that way. Too bad the reverend hadn't been inspired to help out the troubled situation with a little bit of old-fashioned preaching on brotherly love.

Grace depressed the intercom button on her desk to call Bonnie Stucki, the school secretary.

"Bonnie, were you able to set up that appointment with Mr. Henshaw for me this afternoon?"

"Yes, I was, Mrs. Banner. It's scheduled for four o'clock."

"Great!"

"Uh, well, maybe not so great. He was complaining about some broken pop bottles he found on his lot."

"What makes him think our schoolchildren had anything to do with that?"

"I think he just hates kids, Mrs. Banner."

"And I was going to try and talk to him again about us using his lot for a school playground for the rest of the school year."

"I don't think that's going to happen, do you?"

"Not without a miracle," agreed Grace. "I've got my paperwork caught up here. I'll be in Miss Hopkins's class if you need me, Bonnie."

"Right, Mrs. Banner. Oh, I called Mr. Hollister and scheduled an appointment for him with you. I know you've been trying to set up a conference with him, so I told him you had some free time during today's lunch hour. I hope that's all right."

"That's fine, Bonnie." Grace released the intercom

button, uncomfortable with the tiny spark of excitement she experienced at hearing Matthew's name. It was unnerving to have to remind herself their conversation today would be strictly business. The business of how her son detested his son—and vice versa.

She smoothed the lapels of her white suit and regretted her rush this morning when she'd dressed. She was vain enough to wish she'd chosen something beside the outfit he'd seen her in at church yesterday.

As she left her office, Grace couldn't help wondering if there really had been a weekend. After church Sunday, she and a subdued Jason had spent the rest of the day at his grandparents' home where he had nursed his grudge against Brian.

During their visit with Blake's parents, Matthew Hollister's name had come up more than once. Grace had paid very close attention to Dawson Banner's words about his son's former political opponent. She had been surprised to discover the former senator thought of Matthew Hollister more as a member of an opposing football team than as a true enemy. Unfortunately her ten-year-old son seemed unable to make that distinction.

One disturbing statement Blake's father had made continued to nag at Grace. He'd said that, as a boy growing up on the Point, Matthew Hollister had always looked "hungry" to him. Not hungry for food, the older man had clarified. But hungry for recognition. Matthew Hollister had been a natural-born competitor, and he'd chosen Blake Banner as the yardstick on which to measure his boyhood ambitions.

Blake's father had gone on to say that Matthew Hollister was the best thing that had happened to his son. Blake might never have pushed himself to his full potential without Matthew's always trying to equal or surpass his accomplishments. According to Dawson Banner, the finest young men the Point had produced were Matthew Hollister and Blake Banner.

Grace thought about Jason and Brian. They were too young to get locked into the kind of competitiveness that had plagued their fathers. Despite what Dawson had said about the benefits of such rivalry, she shuddered at the possibility of it visiting the next generation of Banners and Hollisters. There was something faintly unhealthy about two boys always trying to best each other. She thought of a young and "hungry" Matthew Hollister and shuddered again. For some reason, her imagination imbued that hunger with a predatory cast.

She shifted her thoughts to the ups and downs of the past couple of days and decided it had not been a red-letter weekend. Except for the accidental encounters with Matthew Hollister. Somehow those random meetings stood out in stark contrast to the normal, muted pattern of her life in Banner's Point.

She didn't understand why, but she'd been thinking a lot about Blake in the past couple of days. It had been more than six years since his death. Why was she suddenly preoccupied with his memory? She knew she didn't have to look far for the answer to that question. And she supposed it was natural that

Matthew Hollister's return to the Point would stir up a lot of old memories.

It was the nature of those memories that she had found disturbing. She was remembering what it felt like to be held by a man, loved by a man. She hadn't known the ache of physical desire in years. None of her casual dates had awakened such feelings within her.

Grace realized that her disquiet stemmed from more than feelings of physical need. She had remembered just what kind of marriage she and Blake had had. At the time she supposed it had satisfied both of them. But she wasn't the woman she'd been six years ago, and she recognized that she would expect much more now both emotionally and physically than Blake had ever given her.

And despite the uneasiness Dawson Banner's words about Matthew's past competitiveness with Blake had aroused, she sensed on an intuitive, feminine level that Matthew would be capable of providing a nurturing love for the woman in his life. She remembered the last days of the congressional election, when it had become obvious that his pregnant wife was gravely ill. He had cut back his speaking engagements to spend time with the ailing woman. Most political experts had said his dwindling campaign appearances had cost him the closely contested election.

Ancient history, she reminded herself, taking a deep breath and filling her lungs with the scents of mimeograph fluid and floor wax. As she walked down the empty corridor toward the gym, her gaze wandered over the Halloween pictures decorating the pale green walls. She had to smile at the children's vivid portrayals of witches, ghosts and goblins. Imagination and creativity were certainly in no short supply.

And as usual for October, the children were bursting with anticipation. Their high spirits didn't disturb her in the least. She liked the excitement filling the air. It was a fun time for everyone at Peninsula Elementary.

She pushed open the door to the gymnasium and scanned the high-beamed room. At precisely 3:30 p.m. on Halloween, she and Floyd Brinton, the school custodian, would oversee the evacuation of fifty-four student desks so the gym could be prepared for the annual Halloween carnival.

The school board and community used the excuse of raising money to hold the carnival. But the truth was, parents as well as children enjoyed the good times provided by the celebration.

Grace noticed that only half of the desks in the gym were presently occupied. In one section of the vast room, Miss Hopkins had erected two dozen easels. Twenty-four intense young artists, wearing oversize shirts to protect their clothes, wielded brushes dripping with paint as they slaved over their masterpieces.

"Well, what's your professional opinion, Miss Hopkins? Do we have any budding geniuses in our fifth-grade class this year?"

"Of course," replied the teacher with a smile.

Grace's gray eyes sparkled. "I like your attitude."

Miss Hopkins's smile widened. "Come see the children's projects. I think you'll be impressed."

Grace turned her attention to the students working industriously at their desks. She walked slowly between the rows, pausing occasionally to study the unusual creations. Peering over Carmen Rodriguez's shoulder, Grace stopped.

"What are you making, Carmen?"

"It's going to be a collage," answered Carmen, looking at the couple of hundred brightly dyed macaroni noodles spread over a large sheet of orange construction paper. An open bottle of white glue rested near her elbow.

"It looks like you're really working hard on it, Carmen."

The girl nodded. "I cut out these pieces of colored paper and Mrs. Hopkins gave me the beads."

Grace looked at the intricately cut shapes of different colored construction paper and realized Carmen had probably spent hours on her project. The gaudy beads in the shoe box on her desk must have come from more than a dozen costume jewelry necklaces.

"Your collage is really going to be special, Carmen. We'll have to display it in a place of honor at the carnival."

Carmen glowed at the praise. "Thank you, Mrs. Banner. Brian Hollister let me use his desk while he painted today because his desk is bigger than mine. I needed the extra room for my bead box."

Grace's eyes sought Brian as he stood like a miniature Picasso before his canvas of dripping oranges and blacks. Evidently the Hollister men started young when it came to attracting the female of the species. Her gaze moved to Jason standing at an easel not more than four feet away. Uh-oh, only four feet apart and both armed with dripping paintbrushes.

Miss Hopkins was living dangerously—especially with one of her teaching assistants spending the day at the area library conference and the other assistant out of commission with the flu. Grace understood Miss Hopkins hadn't wanted to deny her students the promised project, but most teachers would have postponed the activity until they had ample adult backup.

Grace continued to move quietly among the desks. She was amazed by the variety of tiny objects the students had brought to make their collages. There were jars of beans, boxes of leaves, shoelaces, jacks, feathers, fishing lures, buttons, baubles and bits of lace. Little fingers busily cut, arranged and pasted in silent harmony.

She was just about to compliment Miss Hopkins on her courage and imagination when Carmen's shrill scream ricocheted through the gym.

"Awww!" she shrieked, leaping from Brian's desk as if she'd been shot. Beads, construction paper, gummy white glue and frogs flew in every direction.

Frogs! Grace's cry joined the rising roar as boys and girls jumped from their desks, unleashing hundreds of tiny missiles and great gobs of glue. In horror, Grace watched as the escalating pandemonium moved like a wave toward the easels.

A half dozen croaking frogs hopped in different

directions. Boisterous boys dashed after the creatures, bumping into screaming girls who ran into the center of the gym. Desks, easels and paints were knocked from the path of the thundering herd.

Gamely ignoring the welfare of her white suit, Grace plunged into the middle of the burgeoning riot. "Calm down! They're just frogs!" she shouted, trying futilely to be heard above the children's shrieks. "Don't panic. We'll catch them!"

Just then Brian Hollister let out a hearty yell. "I caught one. Look, Mrs. Banner." The proud boy ran to her, a bug-eyed frog cupped in his hands.

A foot away, his tennis shoes hit a giant puddle of beads. Brian swung his arms madly, trying to recover his balance. Instead he landed on the polished hardwood floor with a loud thump. The frog went flying through the air, its flight stopped by the front of Grace's yellow silk blouse.

Grace gasped and tried to shake the slimy creature off.

"Good Lord!" boomed an astonished male voice.

Matthew Hollister's arrival didn't even register with Grace. She was too busy trying to rid herself of the frog without actually touching it.

Matthew quickly stepped forward and detached the frog from her blouse. "Relax, Grace, I've got it. You're all right."

A comforting arm settled around her shoulders, and she sagged against him. "You run one heck of a school, Principal Lady," he observed softly as he cradled her next to him, absorbing the unrestrained chaos erupting all around them.

Despite the pandemonium, Grace noticed that Matthew Hollister felt awfully good—solid, manly and protective. He smelled good, too—like sunshine, citrusy after-shave and man.

Then his words registered. Resolutely Grace straightened her spine and withdrew herself from the sanctuary of his powerful arms. It was time she took charge of the crisis. Warily she eyed Matthew's large right hand. In it, she knew he held the truant frog.

She drew a steadying breath and surveyed the situation. Miss Hopkins stood comforting Carmen Rodriguez. Six boys held noisy frogs. All but one of the easels had been tipped over. Beads, macaroni and assorted objects lay spilled in puddles of glue and paint. In short, things were under control but messy, very messy.

"All right now," she began quietly. "I want those frogs taken out of here and…" She floundered for a moment. She'd always hated frogs—slimy, clammy and loathsome things. As a little girl, she'd known the unfortunate frog prince would still be sprouting warts if she'd been the princess in the story. But it seemed heartless to have them murdered in cold blood. She glanced at Matthew and read his awareness of her predicament in his amused expression.

"And," she continued determinedly, "let them loose in the vacant lot across the street." She stepped toward the last standing easel. "Now, I want to know who was responsible for bringing the frogs into the gym.''

There was silence all around. Matthew quietly scooped up a battered shoe box from the gym floor. He dropped his captured frog into it, pressing a crumpled lid tightly against it while he motioned the boys holding the other frogs to come forward and deposit them inside. It was done in silence. Not one fifth-grader came forward to own up to the disaster.

Grace's wide gray eyes scanned the room, moving across the pale boys and girls. Her assessing gaze halted at the slumped posture of her son. Jason didn't return her stare, and suddenly Grace remembered the couple of hours he had spent sulking at his grandparents' house Sunday afternoon. The pond behind their home was a notorious breeding place for frogs.

''Carmen, you were the first one to see the frogs. Where were they?''

''In...in Bri-Brian's desk,'' the girl stammered, still shaking.

Matthew Hollister stiffened and leveled a searching look at his son. Grace could tell he wanted to ask Brian a few pointed questions, but refrained from doing so. She appreciated his forbearance.

''Brian, do you know how the frogs got into your desk?''

''No, Mrs. Banner,'' he answered in a straightforward manner.

''What about you, Jason? Do you know how the frogs got into Brian's desk?''

''I guess I do, Mom—er, Mrs. Banner.''

"And?" she pressed resolutely, knowing how disturbing it was for Jason to have to answer her questions in front of the entire fifth grade. She steeled herself against his embarrassment. She refused to play favorites. She couldn't afford to if she wanted to do her job right. Tonight she'd commiserate with Jason over the debacle.

"I put them in Brian's desk," he replied in a shaky voice.

Her heart went out to him as his eyes filled with tears at the calamity his reckless action had unleashed. "Well, Jason, you've got a big mess to clean up."

His young chin came up as she stated the punishment she felt his irresponsibility warranted. The other boys and girls eyed him sympathetically. She was aware that, despite the damage Jason had caused to their art projects, their loyalties fell with one of their own.

The loud buzzer heralding lunch vibrated throughout the gym. "All right, you're excused for lunch." Following Miss Hopkins's lead, the children quietly filed out.

When Jason drew alongside of Grace, she reached out and touched his shoulder. "Not you, Jason. We need to talk."

"I'm sorry, Mom," he said, his voice unnaturally high. "I just thought it would be funny for Brian to find some frogs in his desk. I didn't think any of this would happen."

"I know you're sorry, honey," she said gently.

"But someone is going to have to clean up this mess."

"I'll help him, Mrs. Banner," offered Brian, stunning both adults with his generous offer.

"Were you responsible for any of this, son?" asked his father.

"Maybe, in a way," Brian admitted nervously.

"Explain yourself," ordered his father in a no-nonsense tone.

"Ah, last week I put a bunch of worms in Jason's desk."

"I didn't hear anything about that," said Grace.

"Well, ah…Jason just took them outside without telling on me."

"Then Jason was trying to pay you back for the trick you played on him. I think you're right, son. You do need to help Jason clean this mess up. And then I want to talk to you. These childish pranks are going to stop before someone gets hurt."

Taking a step back, Matthew Hollister turned from the wide-eyed boys to further assess the degree of disaster their feud had wrought. Grace glanced at him and sensed more than saw him stagger. Her eyes darted downward, and she watched in a combination of disbelief and horror as the rugged man struggled to retain his footing on the same patch of shiny beads that had caused his son to trip. Instinctively she reached to offer her support, but her gesture came seconds too late.

Matthew Hollister's feet slid outward, and he crashed hard to the floor, pulling her with him. Nylon-clad limbs entangled with powerful male legs. Together they knocked over the remaining easel, and black and orange poster paint splattered over both of them.

Grace looked up into Matthew's stunned features. His firm lips parted.

"Well, damn, Grace," he growled huskily. "I think I just broke my leg."

Chapter Four

The drive from Peninsula Elementary to the Seventeenth Street Emergency Treatment Center in Idaho Falls took exactly twelve minutes. Without a man seated next to her complaining that his leg was broken, the trip would have taken twice that time. It was amazing what a state of old-fashioned panic could accomplish. Grace hadn't missed a single traffic light. But then, she hadn't been particular as to the color of the light she'd driven through.

One would think Matthew Hollister would have appreciated her efforts in his behalf, thought Grace as she sat in the small waiting area of the emergency facility. Instead, the ungrateful man had threatened to jump from the car if she ran one more stop sign. He didn't accept her rationalization that she hadn't actually *run* the stop signs. She'd slowed down, looked both ways and then just sort of scooted through the intersections.

She glanced at the slim silver watch on her wrist and frowned. More than twenty minutes had passed since the nurse had helped Matthew Hollister into the examining room.

Unable to sit still any longer, Grace rose from the low cushioned bench and approached the admitting secretary. "Do you know if Mr. Hollister broke any bones?"

"We won't know that until Dr. Ford has a look at the X rays," replied the older woman.

"Oh."

"It might make the time pass faster for you if you filled out these forms."

"I'm afraid I can't be of much help to you. I'm the principal at Peninsula Elementary, and Mr. Hollister is the father of one of our students. The accident happened at the school."

"What caused it?"

Grace recounted the incredible incident to the secretary. Midway through her story, she realized the woman was having difficulty keeping a straight face. Grace supposed there was some humor to the situation, but she wasn't in a position to appreciate it.

"Do you know Mr. Hollister's address?" asked the secretary, her pen poised over a daunting stack of medical forms.

"No, I don't even know his—wait a minute," she interrupted herself. "He gave me his business card with his phone number written on the back of it." She fished around in her purse for a moment. "Here it is."

After handing the card to the secretary, Grace slipped into the rest room and, as best she could, sponged the orange and black spots decorating the formerly white suit. It quickly became apparent that her efforts were futile. The outfit was ruined. Grace returned to the waiting room and began to pace. She wondered if Matthew Hollister was the kind of man who believed in lawsuits.

Almost an hour later, a tight-faced Matthew limped into the reception area. His features were set grimly, and he looked pale. His lips were drawn together in a tight line, but his dark eyes reflected wry acceptance instead of the anger Grace had anticipated. His right pant leg was rolled midway up his muscular calf and he wore a thick bandage on his foot. One large hand held a black leather shoe. Grace consoled herself with the fact that he hadn't been put into a plaster cast up to his hip.

A balding, diminutive, white-coated doctor followed him into the room. "Even though it's a simple sprain, you're going to have to take it easy on that foot. You're going to be feeling some pain, so I want you to get this prescription filled." The rotund man scribbled on a pad.

"And I don't want you hobbling around. That's why I'm not prescribing crutches. Settle yourself in an easy chair and elevate that foot. Baby it for a couple of days. You'll be better off in the long run if you don't push yourself."

The doctor slapped his silent patient on the back

and returned to the examining room. Grace rose, going automatically to assist Matthew.

He leaned heavily on her shoulder and muttered under his breath, "Feel like a damned fool."

"Before you leave, Mr. Hollister, we need some information from you." The secretary straightened the ominous pile of forms.

Grace helped Matthew get to the counter. As he leaned against her shoulder, she was again impressed by the hard strength his rugged body radiated. "I'll drive the car closer to the entrance so you won't have to walk so far."

"Just remember to stop before you hit the building," he muttered gruffly.

"Yes, sir," Grace replied softly. "I'll drive you home ever so slowly."

His dark eyes snagged hers and his lips parted in an amused smile. "See that you do. My body's taken enough abuse today. I'm getting to old for all this excitement."

Unwillingly her eyes were drawn across the length and breadth of his manly physique. Old? No way. Every square inch of him consisted of hard contours. From his broad, muscular chest covered with a paint-dappled shirt to the navy slacks emphasizing his flat stomach and powerful thighs, he was the embodiment of a male animal in its prime. She swallowed. Prime had never looked or smelled so good.

"Grace..." Her name was a hoarse whisper on his lips.

Her gaze shot upward. She expected to see pain

mirrored in his dark eyes. Instead, she found a smoldering hunger that took her breath away.

"Get the car."

While she drove a somber Matthew Hollister back to Banner's Point, a growing tension filled her white Buick sedan. Made self-conscious by her blatant physical awareness of his maleness, she kept her eyes pinned to the road. Nor did her silent companion seem inclined to break the quiet pressing in at them from all sides.

Grace reached out and flicked on the radio. The strains of a Chopin waltz embraced them. Somehow, the haunting melody seemed to heighten instead of diminish her awareness of the man beside her. Strange thoughts danced through her mind.

Was there a woman in Matthew Hollister's life? Did he intend on settling permanently in Banner's Point? Did women with brown hair and gray eyes appeal to him? What would it feel like to be kissed by—

A lean forefinger reached over and shut off the radio. "This is as good as place as any."

Grace's head jerked around, and she stared at him in confusion. "Here?"

"Sure, this place has a prescription department, doesn't it?"

He pointed to the discount store they were approaching.

Grace nodded and pulled into the store's huge parking lot. "I won't be long."

"I hate to put you to the trouble, but I'd better follow the doctor's orders."

She glanced at her injured passenger. Something in his voice alerted her to the fact he was uncomfortable. She reached for her purse. "It's no trouble," she assured him.

"I don't usually bother with medication," he informed her with studied casualness.

All at once Grace knew what Matthew Hollister's problem was. Like most men, he hated admitting he was human enough to need a painkiller.

"If it would make you feel better, I could stop in sporting goods, too."

He raised a dark brow. "Why sporting goods?"

"Why, to buy you a bullet to bite," she replied sweetly.

Matthew chuckled softly, his gaze sweeping across her flushed face and then dropping to examine the rest of her. He was tempted to tell her that ever since they'd fallen together on the gym floor, he'd been entertaining fantasies about biting *her*—albeit gently. She had damned enticing earlobes.

"Don't be a smart aleck. Just get the pills and take me home."

"I'll be back before you know I've gone." She flashed him a smile as fresh and warm as a sunrise in June.

The focus of his thoughtful eyes followed her across the parking lot. Too bad, he thought with a grimace of pain as he repositioned his bandaged foot. Too bad he would never discover how that sunshiny smile tasted. A scowl darkened his rough-cut features. He was getting awfully tired of the gut level attraction he felt toward the primly beautiful Grace Banner.

Nevertheless, images of her piquant beauty filled his mind. Her wide gray eyes could snap with fire, widen with innocent amazement and then shine with humor in the space of mere seconds. Her soft, full lips seemed to invite fantasies of long, sultry nights and her body... Oh, she was made for loving, all right. But not for just one night.

No, Grace Banner's pureness of spirit shone through her delicate beauty as clearly and brightly as the sun piercing a silver cloud. Matthew Hollister knew the elementary-school principal was as honest, dedicated and wholesome as she could be. He just couldn't figure out how she managed to look so damned sexy.

His scowl deepened. Her sexiness was beside the point. As far as he was concerned, Grace Banner simply wasn't his kind of woman. She couldn't be. Not when she was so utterly different in temperament from the boisterous, irreverent woman Cathy had been. And he'd been happy with Cathy. It stood to reason that if—and that was a mighty big if—he became serious about another woman, she would have to be a lot like his first wife.

When he realized the direction his thoughts had taken, he swallowed a soft oath. It didn't matter that Grace and Cathy had diametrically opposed personalities. Grace had been married to Blake Banner. That simple, irrevocable fact obliterated any possibility of a shared future for the two of them.

And if he admitted to himself that, despite her having been married to Blake, he *was* attracted to her? The admission changed nothing. There was still too much history between them. The Banners and Hollisters had a tradition of being on opposite sides. As Matthew stared out the car window, he pondered what a poor bedfellow reality made.

Grace slanted Matthew a sideways glance. His mouth was a rigid slash across his grim features, his dark brows were drawn together in concentration and his eyes stared unseeingly ahead. He had remained silent throughout the return trip to Banner's Point. Obviously he was in pain.

"We could stop and you could take a pill now," Grace suggested.

"I'm fine."

His terse response discouraged further conversation. And yet, since she was sure he was in physical pain, Grace took no offense. Minutes slipped by.

"I'm sorry, I didn't mean to snap at you," came a low growl from her passenger.

"It's all right. I understand." She wasn't sure, but she thought he uttered a low-voiced oath. Again silence stretched between them.

Despite the impossibility of his ever becoming intimately involved with Grace Banner, Matthew discovered he couldn't keep his fascinated gaze from studying her delicate features. Any lipstick she'd worn was now gone from her soft lips. He assumed she used makeup, but it had been so subtly applied he couldn't detect its presence.

His gaze dropped to where her hands gripped the steering wheel. Clear polish adorned her neatly manicured nails. He frowned at the ornate diamonds that decorated her slender ring finger. The elaborate settings seemed too heavy for her. Had he selected her jewelry, he would have picked something more in proportion with her delicate bone structure.

"How do you feel about Brian and me moving back to the Point?" It was the one question he'd had no intention of asking, yet hearing her response was suddenly crucial to him.

"Why *did* you come back, Matthew?"

He studied her profile, aware she hadn't answered his question. "I was losing Brian."

"I don't understand."

"I'd gotten sucked in, Grace. To the power trip of running a national multimillion-dollar corporation. To fifteen-hour workdays. To business trips taking me all over the country. Without realizing it, I was seriously neglecting my son."

"You're being hard on yourself."

"I deserve it. Oh, I told myself everything I did was for Brian and his future, but that was a bunch of bull. I was doing it for me and the charge I got from being a big-shot business executive."

"What happened to change your priorities?"

A shadow of pain crossed Matthew's features. "A good friend of mine had a son two years older than

Brian. The boy became addicted to some pretty ugly drugs.''

''That's terrible.''

''He died, Grace. Twelve years old and his life was finished. My friend is never going to get over it.'' Matthew's deep voice shook with emotion.

The muscles in Grace's throat constricted. ''A loss like that…''

''I know moving Brian was a drastic step. But I couldn't trust myself not to get back on that fifteen-hour-a-day treadmill.''

''Are you retiring?''

Matthew smiled. ''That drastic a step I'm not ready for. Right now I'm on vacation.''

Grace heard the irony in his deep voice and spared him a brief glance. ''Working in your father's garage seems a peculiar way to spend a vacation.''

''When I took the time off from D.D., it was to give me a chance to get closer to Brian. Dad and Mom already had their reservations for a cruise along the Mexican coast.''

''Now that sounds like a vacation.''

''Second honeymoon,'' Matthew corrected lightly. ''Though I don't think they really ever had a first one. Mom and Dad have worked hard their whole lives. Anyway, when the man Dad hired to run the shop while they were away changed his mind at the last minute, I volunteered to fill in.''

''I bet they appreciated that.''

Matthew chuckled. ''Mom did, but Dad wasn't

convinced I'd be willing to get my hands dirty. A lot of years have gone by since I was his ace mechanic.''

The affection and loyalty in Matthew's words made Grace's estimation of him climb. Not only was he a devoted father but he was also a caring son.

''Turns out Dad knew me better than I thought,'' continued Matthew. ''I remembered myself being a whole lot better mechanic than I am. And Dad hasn't modernized the garage over the years. He's slowing down. Retirement isn't too far away for him. Right now his work load is lighter than I ever remember it being.''

''Then you won't be working at the garage after he gets back?''

''No, I'll be concentrating on moving the national headquarters of D.D. to Idaho Falls.''

Grace smiled. ''Has the city's Chamber of Commerce initiated proceedings to have you canonized?''

His lips curved upward. ''Not that I know of, but I could probably get them to put a statue of me next to that fifty-foot Indian they've got on the North Gate Mile. Where did that come from?''

''A few years ago a man who carved Indians from huge tree trunks came through town. He used a chain saw to rough it out and then finished it by hand.''

''I've never seen anything like it.''

''It is rather impressive.'' Grace slid Matthew an amused glance. ''Maybe the city fathers will invite him back to immortalize you in tree trunk.''

''Half the citizens of Banner's Point would probably sneak into Idaho Falls one night and burn it to the ground.''

Immediately Grace sobered. ''Have you encountered a lot of hostility since you moved back?''

''More than I ever expected. I can't believe how many people are still harping on that damned campaign. It's been ten years.''

Grace felt her cheeks flush as she remembered her own initial antagonism toward Matthew. ''I guess some people find it hard to let go of the past.''

''Do you resent me for running against Blake?''

Why did answering him honestly make her feel as if she were somehow betraying Blake's memory? ''I think it's time people forgot about that election. It's been ten years. There comes a point when you have to let go of the past.''

''Let go of the past... It's never easy, is it?''

All at once Grace had the feeling they were no longer discussing a rough political campaign. ''No, it's never easy, but it is necessary.''

''How long has it been since Blake died?''

Forever. ''Six years.''

''It's been nine years since Cathy died.''

His voice was flat, and Grace wondered about the women he must have known since his wife's death. That he had not remarried was a strong indication he was content to spend the rest of his life uncommitted to one woman. He was probably quite adept at handling temporary liaisons.

''It's starting to snow,'' Matthew observed softly, gesturing toward the dry, powdery flakes that had begun to filter down from the grayish sky. "Looks like winter's finally come to Idaho."

"Yes, it does."

"This is going to be quite a change for Brian and me. A whole three months of winter."

"*Three* months? Oh, Matthew, you've been away from Banner's Point too long."

"I have?"

She nodded. "You've forgotten we suffer a full five months of icky, icy, snowy and generally yucky weather."

"What happened to the joys of ice skating, building snowmen, skiing, snowmobiling, horse-drawn sleighs—"

"Horse-drawn sleighs?"

"My dad has a team of trained horses."

"Well, you've got five months to enjoy them."

"I guess I have been away from the Point too long, but I intend to make up for lost time."

Grace turned off at the exit to the Peninsula, braking when a huge porcupine began to lumber across the highway.

Matthew chuckled. "Snow and porcupines. It's great being back here."

"Has the Point changed much while you've been away?"

"Would you believe not a bit? Brewster's Hardware, Julene's Diner, the Brinkwaters' mom and pop grocery store, May's Beauty Parlor, the potato-packing plant and Hollister's Auto Repair. Lord, you can't believe what a charge I got the first time I drove down Main Street again.''

Matthew Hollister's enthusiasm touched a responsive chord within Grace. ''Don't forget the city building and the school.''

''Yeah, it's all still here. And for some dumb reason I can't begin to understand, I'm glad.''

''I'm glad too,'' she said softly, wondering at the warm satisfaction flooding through her at his words.

''Turn left on First Street. I bought the old Robinson house.''

The Robinson house was a three-story mansion that overlooked the Snake River and was situated in a thicket of century-old pines. It was one of the five mansions that had been built in the early 1900s on the southern side of the Peninsula. Blake's parents' home was another of the five and the Banners were Matthew's nearest neighbors.

She drove up the circular gravel drive to the wide double doors framed by twin white pillars and stopped. Surely Matthew Hollister and his son didn't live alone in the huge home. He had to have at least a housekeeper and just maybe a live-in girlfriend. For the first time since moving to Banner's Point, Grace wished she were plugged in to the local network of friendly gossips. They would know everything there was to know about Matthew Hollister's living arrangements.

Grace opened her car door and went around to assist Matthew up the wide porch.

"That's all right. I think I can make it in under my own power."

She scanned the intimidating steps before returning her gaze to Matthew. Feminine amusement sparkled in her gray eyes. "I don't think you're in any position to be turning down help."

One side of his mouth curved into a rueful smile. "I guess you're right."

The inside of the old Robinson house reminded Grace of her in-laws' home. It had a Victorian-style entry, high ceilings, polished wood floors and vividly dyed Oriental rugs. She helped Matthew to a high-backed, brick-red velvet chair, noticing that a fine layer of moisture bathed his forehead. His eyes closed.

"Shall I get you a glass of water so you can take a pain pill?"

"I'd appreciate it." He spoke without opening his eyes. "The kitchen is down the hall and to your left."

Grace quickly located the glasses and filled one with water. It took a couple of moments for her to pry the stubborn lid off the child-resistant bottle of pills the pharmacist had given her. Then she hurried back to the living room and offered Matthew two small white tablets.

"Thanks." He washed down the pills with several swallows of water and gave the glass back to her.

She retraced her steps to the kitchen, rinsed out the tumbler and then returned to the living room. Matthew didn't look any too comfortable in the high-backed chair.

"Could I help you to the couch, Matthew? It would be easier to prop up your foot. The doctor did say you should elevate it."

"That probably would be more comfortable." He leaned forward, and Grace helped him up. Together they bridged the short distance to the sofa. "Why don't you push the coffee table closer?"

She did so and then placed one of the sofa pillows on the low table to cushion the weight of his bandaged foot. Without analyzing her action, she reached forward with her fingertips to smooth his brow. It was a wholly spontaneous act, one that seemed as natural to her as her next breath.

But Matthew Hollister's dark eyes snapped open and captured her with hot intensity. Before she could even think of reacting, a powerful hand snaked out to catch her by the wrist. Stunned by his swiftness, she stared down at him with huge eyes.

For a timeless moment their gazes locked. Confusion, anger and desire seemed to chase across Matthew's grim features. Then, with a forceful tug, he pulled her onto his lap. And suddenly there was no time to decipher her own feelings, let alone his.

Powerful arms gathered her close to him, and all at once his entire body embraced hers. Fire seemed to spiral out of control inside her, racing toward the answering heat of his hard, virile body.

Grace's wide gray eyes could only gaze in wonder at the firm, male mouth hovering a breath from her parted lips. And then as she acknowledged an impulse as ancient as the man-woman need that drove them, her slender arms encircled his corded neck and she pulled his head to hers.

The warm pressure of his mouth as it moved gently across hers created a yearning within her so sweetly powerful that Grace felt tears gather behind her closed eyelids. Oh, this was right, she thought dazedly. This was so, so right!

She pressed herself against him, deepening a kiss that had started out as a cautious testing between them. She felt as if she were drawing his strength inside her. And all the time, she knew. She knew in some quiet, sane part of her that it was she, not he, who had become the aggressor. But it had been so long! Too long. Forever.

The thud of his heart against her breasts, the fierce ardor of his embrace and the raw hunger their kiss awakened tore at the cold shell of loneliness that had held her prisoner for six long years, for a lifetime.

"Grace, Grace, Grace," he groaned, his strong hands gripping her shoulders as he gently pushed her from him. "This is a mistake."

It took a moment for Matthew's hoarsely uttered words to penetrate Grace's passion-dazed thoughts. When they did, they cut through her with the force of machine-gun fire. Frantically, she mentally replayed the previous few minutes. Had she thrown herself at him? A furious blush singed her skin as she tried to dislodge herself from his lap.

Then, it dawned on her. *He'd* pulled her down to *his* lap. *He'd* planted a blistering kiss on her mouth. Only it hadn't been blistering. Not at first. No, at first it had been warm and tender—and the most wonderful kiss of her entire life. She'd been the one who'd slipped over the edge of control and demanded more than the simple warmth and tenderness he'd offered.

"Stop wiggling," rasped Matthew, feeling terribly noble for stopping things before they could get out of hand. But he didn't know how much longer he could continue behaving nobly with Grace squirming across his lap.

"I'm trying to get off you," she protested, both infuriated and mortified by the fact her voice was quavering and the hem of her skirt had sneaked up to her hips.

"Just a minute, and I'll—"

In her present state of mind any delay was too much. With more haste than grace, she hopped from his lap.

"Ow!"

"Oh, Lord, I'm sorry, Matthew," Grace cried, staring remorsefully at the bandaged foot that had slipped from its resting place during their tussle. She quickly knelt and retrieved the pillow, inserting it beneath his injured foot.

"It's…" He drew a deep breath. "It's all right, Grace. I probably deserved it for grabbing you. Anyway, I'm the one who should be apologizing." He looked up from the couch with a chagrined expression.

"Yes, you should," agreed Grace, backing away warily. Just what kind of magic did this charismatic man possess?

"Uh…" He cleared his throat. "Well then, thank you for the ride home and filling the prescription for me."

"You're welcome." She wanted nothing more than to be away from this man and his very real power over her.

Yet she stood quietly beside the couch, waiting for him to bring his labored breathing under control. For despite the temporary madness they'd shared, they had to maintain a civilized relationship in order to solve the problem with their warring sons.

Briefly their eyes met. His held confusion and the smoldering embers of passion left unsatisfied. Hers held the same confusion and the rawness of newly awakened hunger. Then, as nothing else could have, the opening and closing of Matthew's front door abruptly jarred them back to their surroundings.

"Dad! Dad! Are you okay?" Brian trotted into the living room.

"Just dandy," replied Matthew, gingerly shifting his throbbing foot upon the pillow.

"Gosh, you really did get hurt, Dad." A tinge of awe colored Brian's voice.

Brian's sober young face moved Grace. This was probably the first time he had seen his father incapacitated. That could be a disturbing experience for a boy his age.

"I'm okay, son. The doctor said I'd be good as new in a couple of days. Come here."

The boy moved to his father's side. Matthew's powerful arms came around his son and he gave him a quick, tight hug. Grace realized Matthew too had read the fear in Brian's eyes and was reassuring him that everything was all right. His perceptiveness and concern brought a tightness to her throat. There was just something incredibly moving about seeing a strong, virile man like Matthew Hollister comforting someone in his arms.

It was hard to believe that moments before she'd been held in those powerful arms and offered the same comfort. Then her body, still humming with errant tingles of excitement, reminded her she'd experienced something more raw and primitive than mere comfort.

Brian straightened. "What's for dinner?"

"I'm afraid it's going to be your cooking tonight, son."

"Yuck!"

"Think how I feel," teased Matthew. "Peanut butter and jelly sandwiches is hardly my idea of dinner."

"Ah, Dad, let's get pizza."

"You driving?" he asked in amusement.

Grace wanted nothing more than to put distance between herself and Matthew Hollister. Yet years of good manners and a strong dose of guilt compelled her to speak up. "Look, I put a roast and potatoes in the crock pot this morning. There's always enough for two meals. It will only take me a minute to run home and bring you back some."

"Super!"

"Wait a minute," protested Matthew, his brows

coming together in a frown. "We can survive one night on peanut butter and jelly."

Remembering clearly that it was her son who was responsible for his injury, Grace insisted, "It's no trouble—really. I'll be back in a few minutes."

"Thanks, Mrs. Banner," interjected Brian before his father could voice a further objection.

Ten minutes later, Grace was rushing through her kitchen, throwing together some odds and ends to complete the dinner she had promised the Hollisters. Leaning against the arched entry to the family room, Jason eyed her hectic efforts with a faint scowl.

"You mean you're going to give our food to *Brian*?"

His hostile voice made food sound like gold and Brian like a no-good claim jumper.

"It's the neighborly thing to do," replied Grace, casting a meaningful glance at her son. "After all, it's our fault Mr. Hollister was injured."

Jason squirmed uncomfortably. "I'm sure sorry about the frogs and all."

"I'm sorry, too. Mr. Hollister hurt his foot very badly and won't be able to work for a week. I think you owe him a personal apology *besides* helping me take dinner to his house."

"All right," Jason mumbled dejectedly.

Grace opened the refrigerator and took out the two chocolate pudding parfaits she'd made that morning. Jason straightened from his slouched position in the doorway.

"Hey, you're not giving Brian my pudding, are you?"

Grace met Jason's indignant green eyes over the top of the fridge door and relented. "No, I won't give away your pudding." She put back the parfait glasses and reached for a covered dish that contained fruit salad.

"Did you and Brian get the gym put back in order?"

"Yeah."

"It was nice of Brian to help you," she observed, placing a can of string beans on the counter beside the salad. She noticed there was no protest against giving away the vegetables.

"I guess so."

"Did Miss Hopkins pass final inspection on the clean-up job?"

"Yeah."

"Good. I don't suppose she assigned any homework tonight?"

Jason's expression brightened. "No."

Despite herself, Grace laughed. "Oh, Jason, come here." She gave her son a quick hug and then stood back and ruffled his hair. "I guess it's been quite a day for you, too."

"You can say that again."

"Grab your coat, hon. It's getting cold outside."

Grace finished assembling the portable meal, taking a minute to butter a couple of slices of bread and put them in a plastic sandwich bag. She looked up when Jason returned. He was struggling with the stubborn zipper of his summer Windbreaker. Its shiny blue fabric was stretched tautly against his solid chest, and the sleeves missed his wrists by a full two inches. It jolted her to see how much he'd grown in just the past few months.

"Looks like I'm going to have to buy you a new coat. I saw a red one at the department store the other day that looked really—"

"I don't want it," interrupted Jason.

"But you haven't even seen it," protested Grace.

"I bet I have. On Brian Hollister."

"Oh." She studied her son's antagonistic expression for a moment before speaking. "Honey, you really haven't given Brian much of a chance to be your friend."

"I don't need him for a friend. I've got plenty of friends."

"Have you thought that maybe he needs you? You were only four when we moved to Banner's Point, so you probably don't remember what it's like to be the new kid in town. It isn't easy, honey. Don't you think you could give Brian a chance before you write him off? He did help you clean the gym, didn't he?"

"Yeah."

"He didn't have to. I'm sure it took a lot of hard work to clean up that mess."

Jason made no reply, and Grace sighed. Boys. Men. It made no difference. Stubbornness must be ingrained into the male of the species at the time of conception.

Chapter Five

The five-minute ride to Matthew's house took place in silence. And though she tried not to, Grace found herself reliving those breathless moments when the hot pressure of Matthew's mouth on hers had obliterated everything from her mind but the touch and feel of him.

Matthew Hollister surely did know how to kiss. Her skin tingled as she realized he probably knew how to do a great deal more than that. And do it well.

Why had he kissed her? And why had she responded as if he were the man of her dreams? Oh, she knew *why*. She wasn't a complete novice with men, after all. There was such a thing as animal magnetism. And desire. But why him? Why Matthew Hollister? If it were any other man, she could explore her feelings and...

But it had been Matthew. It had been Matthew who

had made her feel like a woman again. And it must never happen again. With him.

And why not?

Grace stiffened, her fingers tightening their grip on the steering wheel. The question somehow seemed highly improper. And yet Grace felt compelled to swiftly itemize a list of barriers standing between herself and Matthew.

He had been nothing but trouble to her since his return to the Point. He and her late husband had never gotten along. In fact Matthew had pushed Blake into a rivalry that had lasted for years. It would be utterly disloyal to Blake's memory to become involved with Matthew.

Grace rounded the final curve leading to Matthew's house and eased up on the accelerator. Her chaotic thoughts took a nasty detour. Matthew Hollister had a record of competition with Blake. Just how far did that competitiveness extend? To proving that Blake's widow was his for the taking?

What would it do for Matthew's ego to make love to a woman who had belonged to his rival? Grace braked to a stop and flicked off the headlights. Make love? Matthew had held her, kissed her. Nothing else. Surely in this liberated day and age that didn't constitute making love. Her troubled thoughts conjured up the image of Matthew's roughly hewn features. And she remembered the flicker of sensual awareness she'd felt when he'd taken her hand into his lean, strong one.

With Matthew Hollister, shaking hands could be

construed as making love. Or at any rate foreplay. She reminded herself that he hadn't pushed for anything beyond the kiss. And he'd been the one to draw away first. Besides, he'd been in pain with a badly sprained ankle. The scene had hardly been right for an attempted seduction. She was letting her imagination run away with her. Matthew obviously had no sexual designs on her.

Grace opened the car door, and the overhead light came on. "Jason, you carry in the salad and roast, okay?"

Jason sniffed the casserole dish appreciatively. "When do we get to eat?"

"In a few minutes. We'll just drop off their dinner and then go home."

"Good."

"Jason—"

"I'm starved," he replied innocently as he headed up the front steps.

But it took more than a few minutes to serve the food they'd brought. Mainly because Matthew insisted on limping into the large ranch-style kitchen where Grace unpacked the dinner items. He sat at the round oak table watching her through hooded eyes, and her fingers immediately became thick and clumsy. All she could think about was the time she'd spent in his arms. She darted a glance in his direction. Was he remembering those passionate moments, too?

Then her gaze went to Jason and Brian. The two boys sat across the table, each eyeing the other like a bantam rooster staking out his patch of barnyard turf. Her eyes returned to Matthew. Now he too, was studying the youngsters. Then, as if sensing her stare, he looked up. Rueful humor softened his rugged face. She stepped forward and placed the serving dishes on the table Brian had set.

I know. We've got a real problem on our hands. His speaking gaze seemed to confirm his awareness of Jason and Brian's mutual antagonism.

"So, boys, how's the gym looking?" Matthew inquired quietly.

Jason and Brian jumped at the question. Then they looked at each other, waiting to see who would speak first.

"It's—" They both answered together and then broke off.

Matthew focused his attention on his son. "Brian?"

"We got it all cleaned up."

"Good." Silence greeted his succinct comment.

Grace and both boys sensed Matthew Hollister had more to say on the subject of the day's fiasco and they were not disappointed.

"Now, what are you two boys going to do to make sure nothing like this happens again?" he asked, his deep voice matter-of-fact and yet reeking masculine authority.

Brian responded first. "I'm not going to pull any more tricks on Jason."

"You're right about that, son. How about you, Jason?" Dark eyes bored into Jason's pale face.

"I'm not going to pull any more tricks, either.

And…and, I'm really sorry about your foot, Mr. Hollister.''

Matthew smiled whimsically. "Me too. I accept your apology, Jason, and hope you and Brian can put your feud on ice."

Grace appreciated the fact that Matthew hadn't insisted the boys shake hands or apologize to each other. Their young pride was pretty sensitive. Forcing them to pretend friendship would have been the worst thing to do.

"I understand you're in the church's Webelos pack, Jason."

"Yes, sir."

"You know I'm going to be the new den leader?"

"Yes, sir."

"I'd like for us to be able to work together. Can I count on your cooperation?"

Jason's stormy eyes darted to Brian. "I guess so."

"And you, Brian. Can I count on your cooperation?"

"Yes."

Grace released the breath she'd been holding, feeling as if she'd just witnessed the successful treaty of two warring nations at a summit conference. She reached for her jacket. No sense in giving the two hostile parties time for second thoughts.

"Come on, Jason, we need to go home." Matthew moved as if to stand. "No, please don't try to get up. Jason and I can see ourselves out." She stepped toward the doorway, suddenly conscious of Matthew's pensive eyes. Uncertain of her own mood and feelings, she made a point of avoiding his gaze.

"Thank you, Grace."

She couldn't ignore the quiet intensity of his voice. Against her will, it drew her gaze to his. A dark lock of hair had fallen across his wide forehead, softening his craggy features. As far as Grace was concerned, Matthew Hollister had never looked so appealing. Nor so aloof.

His gaze was as remote as the most faraway star. Had the distant man seated at the table really held her in his powerful arms and claimed her mouth with kisses both hot and hungry? Maybe she'd asked for it. Or maybe she had only imagined it. Maybe... She'd better get the heck out of Matthew Hollister's kitchen.

"You're welcome." She drew a steadying breath, took her son and went home.

"Good night, Mom."

Grace stood at the doorway of Jason's darkened bedroom. Softly she whispered the time-worn phrases she used every night. "Good night, honey. Sleep well."

Morning rituals, nighttime rituals... Later, relaxing in a hot tub full of scented bathwater, Grace pondered the familiar fabric of her life. How much of what she did each day was merely the result of mindless habit? And why did it take the appearance of Matthew Hollister in her life to make her realize she'd been marking time instead of living life to its fullest?

Grace stepped from the tub and enfolded herself in a large coral bath towel. Unexpected thoughts of Matthew made her own body seem unfamiliar to her, and forbidden images darted into her mind. Images of dark, powerful hands caressing pale, sensitive flesh. Resolutely she banished the stirring pictures.

But the memory of the kiss she and Matthew had shared refused to disappear. Again she assured herself the kiss had meant nothing. Nothing more or less than a brief flicker of desire that they would both see was never reignited. Anyway, it hadn't been *his* kiss as much as *hers*.

She'd been the one who'd made the electric contact of their lips into something Matthew had never intended. And he'd responded by calling a halt to the moment of madness. Perhaps the memory of that ill-fated kiss wouldn't be so disturbing if she'd been the first to draw away.

Grace slipped into a pale blue silk nightgown and headed straight for bed. She couldn't remember the last time she'd been as tired as she was tonight. The day's tumultuous events had sapped her small store of reserve energy.

She'd barely gotten settled when the telephone on her nightstand let out a loud ring. Not wanting it to disturb Jason, she grabbed the receiver, berating herself for hoping it would be Matthew Hollister's deep voice on the other end of the line.

"Hello." The huskiness in her voice sounded unfamiliar to her own ears.

"Mrs. Banner, this is Randolph P. Henshaw here, and I think you have one helluva nerve!"

Grace wondered if the day would never end. "What seems to be the problem, Mr. Henshaw?"

"The problem is I can't abide people who don't keep their damned appointments!"

"Oh, dear. I missed our meeting, didn't I?"

"Damned right you did!"

"Please don't swear at me, Mr. Henshaw. There's a perfectly good reason why I didn't—"

"Don't *you* be telling me how to talk, little lady. I've got forty years on you. Don't you teach respect for your elders at that school of yours?"

If he hadn't owned the darned lot across the street from the school, she would have told Randolph P. Henshaw what he could do with his lecture on manners!

"What's the matter? Cat got your tongue?"

"Mr. Henshaw—"

"Not only did you stand me up, lady, you let loose a bunch of frogs on my property. I ought to take you to court."

"I didn't know what else to do with them," she protested faintly.

"Well, ain't that just typical?" Mr. Henshaw said nastily. "City people! Lady, you got frogs, you kill them. Plain and simple. You sure as hell don't transport them to *my* property and let them go!"

"It won't happen again."

"You can bet your fancy new school it won't. 'Cause if you or any of your ragtag kids step foot on my property again, I'll slap your behinds in jail! I'm going to get a restraining order to keep you off my lot.''

A shattering click terminated the call.

Grace returned the receiver to its resting place. The old coot! He'd probably hated school when he was a kid and had waited all these years to get even with the system.

A wave of disappointment washed through her. So much for Mr. Henshaw letting them put playground equipment on his lot. Tomorrow at school she'd have to let Bonnie know she'd been right. Randolph P. Henshaw just plain hated kids—and frogs. Live ones at any rate.

''Bonnie, what time was Ms. Coulson's appointment?''

''She's due any minute, Mrs. Banner.''

''Thank you.'' Grace released the intercom button and reached for the Rodriguez file. The long-term nature of the Rodriguez situation was reflected in the fact that the thick file had remained on her desk since the first day of school.

She thumbed through the familiar pages, a frown wrinkling her brow. Nothing had changed. Mr. Rodriguez was still an out-of-work widower with five school-age children. He still couldn't speak a word of English. At least, according to a copy of the doctor's report, Mr. Rodriguez should have recovered from the back injury he'd received in a car accident in July.

Bonnie's voice came over the intercom. "Ms. Coulson is here."

"Please send her in." Grace pushed back her chair and stood. Enid Coulson had never been one of her favorite people, and she hadn't been looking forward to this session with the forceful social worker.

The woman entered the small office with the ramrod-stiff posture of a drill sergeant. Her arrival seemed to somehow absorb all the room's excess supply of oxygen. Enid's six-foot frame carried a meaty payload of almost two hundred pounds. Shrewd blue eyes bored down at Grace.

"Are you ready to sign the papers?"

Grace motioned to a chair. "Please sit down."

The woman did so, never taking her eyes from Grace's face. "Well?"

"In good conscience, Ms. Coulson, I don't feel the Rodriguez children should be taken from their father and placed in foster homes."

"Then you aren't considering the children's welfare."

"I think I am, Ms. Coulson. Mr. Rodriguez may be temporarily out of work, but he is a good father." Little Carmen Rodriguez's image and that of her brothers and sisters drifted through Grace's thoughts. "His children love him and they love each other. I don't think they should be separated."

"They live in a pigsty. Their father can't speak a word of English. To all intents and purposes, the man's an illiterate. His children would be better off if they were removed from his influence. In short, they are poor people with poor ways.''

''I think their ways are just fine,'' snapped Grace, her composure leaving her. How dared this woman condemn people because they didn't measure up to her narrow view of how a family should live?

''Have you read the medical report on Mr. Rodriguez?''

''Yes.''

''Then you know he's able to work. If he doesn't have a job one month from today, I'm going to initiate the paperwork needed to place his children in foster homes—without your signature.''

The woman stood. Grace also rose. ''You do what you must, but I'm going to recommend the Rodriguez children remain with their father.''

''Good day, Mrs. Banner.'' Ms. Coulson swept from the room in three purposeful strides.

Grace again picked up the Rodriguez file. Mr. Salvador Rodriguez, age thirty-four. Occupation: carpenter, custodian, auto mechanic...

It took only a moment for Grace to locate Matthew Hollister's business card in her purse. But it took considerably longer for her to actually dial his number. There was the little matter of setting aside her reluctance to further intertwine their lives.

Only a clear image of little Carmen's face and the knowledge that Matthew could help the Rodriguez family gave her the necessary courage to reach for the phone. And when his voice vibrated in her ear, Grace drew upon that same courage to present her case to him. She intended to do so in a forthright, uncomplicated way that would not involve them beyond this phone call.

"Hello."

"Matthew, this is Grace. I'm sorry to bother you, what with your injured foot and all, but—"

"That's all right; I was close to the phone."

Somehow his politeness took some of the steam from her planned scenario. "How is your ankle?"

"Hurting but better. I think the doctor's right. If I stay off it for a couple of days, it will heal quickly."

"Oh."

"You don't sound thrilled about my prognosis."

She could hear the quiet laughter in his voice. "It's not that. It's just... Matthew, I know a man who desperately needs a job. He's had experience as an auto mechanic, but I don't know how good a one he is. I do know he's a wonderful father. He's been out of work for five months because of a car accident he was in. The accident wasn't his fault and—"

"Whoa, slow down. I can't keep up with you."

Grace paused to collect her thoughts and slow her runaway pulse. Why did the mere sound of Matthew's voice affect her so powerfully? She shouldn't have called him. She'd been kidding herself that she could put the memory of the brief passion they'd shared into a sealed chamber of her mind.

"Grace?"

"Y-yes?"

"You can go a little faster."

"What?"

"With your reason for calling me. You know, the mechanic who's a wonderful father, but who might not know a lug wrench from a screwdriver."

"Oh, I'm sure he knows that."

"Good."

"But since you're recovering so quickly, you probably don't need someone to fill in for you at the shop."

"Now, there you're wrong. I've got some problems to untangle in Los Angeles and there's no way I'm going to be able to catch up here. Why don't you have your mechanic friend meet me at the garage tomorrow? I'll see how he handles the work that's in progress. If he can do the job, he's hired."

"Oh, Matthew, that's wonderful."

He chuckled softly. "I'm renowned for my general state of wonderfulness."

She couldn't help laughing. "If not your humility?"

"You can't have everything."

I know. Grace swallowed. "Ah, Matthew, there's just one thing you should know about Salvador Rodriguez."

"And that is?"

She detected a sudden wariness in his voice. "He doesn't speak English."

The following silence was big enough for a huge truck to make a U-turn in.

"Just have him at the shop tomorrow afternoon. We'll take it from there."

"Thank you, Matthew."

"You're welcome, Grace."

Another lengthy pause. Obviously it was time to end the call. It went against all reason, but she didn't want to.

"Grace?"

"Yes?"

"Dinner last night was delicious. You're a good cook."

Well, swell! After the explosive kiss they'd shared, all he could compliment her on was being a good cook. She told herself to be grateful he wasn't bringing up their steamy embrace. It was best for all that the kiss, embrace and moment of madness be forever forgotten.

"It was the least I could do after my son crippled you."

"I'm not exactly crippled," he said dryly.

No, you can still kiss like a living legend! "You know what I mean."

"I've hired a housekeeper, so we're no longer in danger of having to subsist on peanut butter and jelly sandwiches."

"That's good."

"There's just one thing…"

"Yes?" This time it was her voice that carried the note of wariness.

"She doesn't start until tomorrow morning."

"I see."

"A man and growing boy can get awful hungry in that length of time."

"Are you not so subtly hinting you'd like me to bring dinner over tonight for you and Brian?"

"I've never been accused of subtlety. I was thinking of ordering a couple of pizzas in town for us. If you don't mind playing delivery service for a night, we could have dinner together."

"You mean the four of us?"

"It might be a way of getting Brian and Jason to realize they're really not cut out to be enemies."

Grace told herself she would give him a polite no. Now was the moment to call a halt to any further involvement between them.

The ensuing pause provoked a question from Matthew. "Do you have other plans?"

"What? Oh, no, it's just that I..." *I think you're dangerous to the state of my emotional health.* Grace knew she couldn't tell him that.

"You what? Have to wash your hair tonight?"

It was the easily detectable thread of male challenge in his husky voice that proved to be Grace's undoing. "I was going to say I have a meeting after school. Jason and I might be a little late, but we'll be happy to play delivery service tonight."

"Brian and I really appreciate it."

"No problem." Grace hung up the phone before she said something she'd later regret.

She depressed the intercom button. "Bonnie, would you have Carmen Rodriguez sent to my office? We're going to be leaving the school for a while. She's going to be my interpreter with her father."

"Will do. Don't forget you've got a four o'clock conference today with the special ed counselor."

"Thanks for the reminder." Grace leaned back in her chair, idly fiddling with a paper clip. When the new school was finished, it would house three special-education classrooms. Despite her earlier discouragement over not getting permission to set up a playground across the street, a distinct feeling of satisfaction washed through her. They were winning the major battles. That was what counted.

In the larger scheme of things, who cared about something as trivial as... All at once, instead of playground equipment, Matthew Hollister's rugged face appeared in her thoughts. Grace had no idea why she was suddenly feeling so abandoned.

"Come on, Jason. You *love* pizza." Grace glanced at her scowling son, who was sitting with two flat cartons of delicious-smelling pizza on his lap.

"So? Does that mean I have to eat it with *Brian*?"

"Mr. Hollister thought it might help if you and Brian spent a little time together."

"He's in my class at school. He goes to my church. He plays soccer on my team. And he's joined my cub scout den." Jason's voice shook with the monumental injustice of life. "I don't want to spend any more time with him. Especially to eat. He'll spoil my appetite."

Grace seriously doubted the person lived who could do that. "Jason, are you holding a grudge over the campaign Mr. Hollister waged against your father? That doesn't sound very fair. Anyway, your father won that election. And when it was over, *he* wasn't bitter about it, nor was Matthew Hollister.''

Grace's own words startled her. For the first time, she remembered that Blake really hadn't held a grudge against Matthew.

"Brian's a geek."

Grace laughed. "A geek doesn't score field goals." Immediately she realized that wasn't the right thing to say.

"If Coach Potter had left me in the game, I could have scored that goal."

"I know, honey. But don't you see Brian needs a chance to fit in, to participate in the things you do?"

They pulled into Matthew's driveway. "Just give him an opening. You might be surprised at what happens."

An hour and sixteen pieces of pizza later, Grace wondered why she'd wasted her breath trying to soften up Jason's opinion of Brian. The only positive thing they'd accomplished by sharing a meal was to prove that no one could indeed spoil her son's appetite.

"I'll be waiting for you in the car, Mom." Jason scooted his chair from the table and headed out the door.

There was no point in calling him back. Brian had gone up to his room ten minutes earlier.

"I guess my idea fell flat."

Grace looked across the table at Matthew. "I wonder."

"Wonder what? It's pretty obvious they're still teed off at each other."

"Has Brian ever mentioned why he doesn't like Jason?"

"No, not directly, but I suspect Brian would be friends with Jason if…" His words dwindled to silence.

"If Jason weren't holding a grudge against him?" suggested Grace quietly.

Matthew's dark eyes softened. "I didn't want to make their antagonism sound like Jason's fault."

"But I think you've cut to the heart of the matter. I think Jason feels he's being disloyal to his father's memory by being friends with Brian."

"Yeah, I've thought of that."

"And there's more."

"What?"

"This is hard for me to say, but I think Jason is wishing he had a father like you. And I think he's feeling awfully guilty for those feelings."

"There's nothing worse than guilt, Grace," said Matthew with quiet intensity, his dark gaze pinning her. "Jason's really having a rough time of it. I never thought our moving back to the Point would cause so many problems."

"I guess we'll just have to learn to live with their hostility."

He shook his head. "No, I don't think it's a good idea to let the boys get into the habit of having enemies. I expect more from Brian than that. And I think

I've come to know you well enough to realize you expect more than that from Jason.''

"But what can we do? We can't make them be friends.''

Matthew regarded her thoughtfully. "Despite how quiet the boys were tonight, I think we did make headway with them.''

"Because they ate the pizza instead of throwing it at each other?''

A slow smile worked its way across his mouth. "It's a start, and we should continue in that direction; we should engineer more ways for them to spend time together outside of school.''

"Why outside of school?''

"Both Brian and Jason are natural leaders, and at school they've got friends who've chosen up sides between them. It's hard to explain, Grace, but when kids pick a leader they want him to be top gun. So you've got two groups of boys who've lined up behind the guy they think is the king of the hill. Believe me those boys won't be eager to see Jason and Brian make peace.''

"You sound like you're speaking from experience.''

His eyes held hers, and his features sobered. "I am.''

She had the feeling Matthew had enlarged the subject beyond their quarreling sons. She couldn't let this opportunity pass to discover his real feelings toward her late husband.

"Was it that way between you and Blake?''

He nodded. "Blake and I were in the same class at school from the first grade through junior high. We didn't look anything alike, but we were pretty much the same height and build—big for our ages. Whenever the class was divided into teams, Blake would be on one side and I would be on the other."

"The teachers wanted to even up the teams," ventured Grace.

"Yeah, I guess so. But something happened between Blake and me. It was like... I don't know." Matthew stared at her. "We both had to win, to be the best. Anyway, that was how I felt."

"And Blake, did he feel that way, too?"

"I'm not sure. Your husband was a remarkable man. He was a superb athlete, smart and really had a handle on dealing with people. Maybe he was too secure to feel the need to compete the way I did."

And Blake had been a Banner, the golden son of the most prominent family on the Point. His father had progressed from state politics to become a United States Senator. It was all the things that Matthew wasn't saying that struck Grace.

After high school, Blake had gone on to college where he'd continued to excel in sports. He'd been the quarterback of his college football team and also its captain. In his junior and senior years, he had been popular enough with his classmates to be elected student-body president. After college had come law school and then a position with a prestigious firm. And ultimately, Blake's congressional victory.

From Blake's father, Grace had learned that after

high school Matthew Hollister had continued to work in his father's auto shop while taking night classes at a junior college. Had he been jealous of Blake's fast-track successes? It seemed impossible that Matthew, with his competitive spirit, could have felt any other way.

"It's taken me a lot of years to achieve that same feeling of security," Matthew continued seriously.

Has it? Have you really buried your rivalry toward my husband? Or do I represent some kind of challenge to you, some kind of trophy?

Shocked at her thoughts, Grace mentally scrambled for the words that would get their conversation back to their sons. "You said something earlier about Jason and Brian spending time together. What did you have in mind?"

"A fishing trip with the Webelos."

"They'll love that, Matthew. But haven't the boys in the pack chosen up sides between Jason and Brian?"

"Yeah, but I don't think the problem's as serious in a group of only ten boys. Anyway, I'm going to use the buddy system. And guess who're going to be assigned as buddies?"

Grace rested an elbow on the table and cradled her chin with the back of her hand. "You're living awfully dangerously, Matthew Hollister."

His mood seemed to lighten. "You know what they say, Grace?" The hint of a smile curved his mouth.

"What?"

"A man's got to do what a man's got to do."

She laughed. "Just what this world needs, one more macho scoutmaster." Then a new thought struck her. "Say, is this going to be one of those early morning events?" Visions of trying to rouse a sleeping Jason at 4:00 a.m. descended on her.

Matthew leaned forward with a disturbing twinkle in his dark eyes. "Fish wake up early."

"So I've been told." And despite the potent presence of the man sitting across the table from her, Grace couldn't suppress an embarrassingly wide yawn.

Sympathy softened his features. "Tired?"

"A little. It's been a long day." Then Grace perked up. "Oh, that reminds me. I visited Mr. Rodriguez today. He's really excited about working at the shop."

"I didn't realize you spoke Spanish."

"I don't. I took along one of his children as a translator. I could excuse one of them tomorrow to translate for you if you think it would help."

"I think I speak enough Spanish for us to get by. My main concern was his being able to answer the telephone. My mother handles that end of the business, and I was filling in for her, too."

"Oh, I didn't think of that."

"It's all right. I have an answering machine. I'll just take it over to the shop."

His consideration touched her. Matthew Hollister had a depth of character and a caring attitude that were really remarkable. Her eyes felt dry, and she blinked to ease the sudden burning sensation she felt.

What would it be like to have a man like that in her and Jason's life? A man whose motives she could trust implicitly?

"You work too hard, Grace."

Before she could deal with Matthew's concern, the blare of her car horn filled the kitchen.

She pushed back her chair and stood. "I have been summoned. See you around, Matthew."

"Grace…"

His deep voice drew her eyes to him. So what else was new? But his darkly earnest expression caught her by surprise.

"I've been thinking about last night, about our kiss."

Her eyes widened and she couldn't have moved if someone had yelled fire.

"It's probably best we forget it ever happened. Don't you agree?"

Grace retreated toward the doorway, realizing it didn't matter what a man's motives were when he made it clear he wasn't interested in her. "Absolutely."

Chapter Six

"**M**om, it's time to get up."

Grace burrowed deeper beneath the covers. She had no idea what time it was, but her body clock was telling her she had more sleep coming to her. And not even her beloved son was going to deprive her of those blissful hours of rest.

"Come on, Mom. You promised."

Without opening her eyes, she forced her mouth to move. "Promised what?"

"That you'd take me over to Mr. Hollister's this morning. You remember. We're going fishing."

"Fishing..." She opened her eyes and blinked against the brightness of the bedside lamp Jason had turned on.

"Yeah, and if we don't hurry, the fish will all be caught before we get there."

"Jason, it's Saturday morning. The fish are probably sleeping in."

Her son stared at her reproachfully.

Grace sighed, surrendering completely to a wave of maternal guilt. "All right, I'll get up."

"When?" he asked skeptically.

"Now," she moaned. "Now, right this very minute."

He didn't budge. *Smart boy.*

She sat up and pushed back her toasty warm blankets. "Run to the kitchen and pour us some juice; I'll be down in a few minutes."

A half hour later, Grace maneuvered her Buick through the predawn darkness toward Matthew Hollister's house. The much-heralded Webelos fishing adventure had arrived—with a glitch or two.

She fought back her fourth yawn in as many minutes, peering tiredly through her windshield. An epidemic of chicken pox had decimated the troop. It turned out that only five of the scouts had already had the illness. Matthew had decided to let the blemish-free and noncontagious boys fish from the small dock on his property. The dock would give them safe access to the Snake River.

Matthew's plan had been operable until the Morgan twins' mother had gone into labor and the boys had been shuttled off to their grandparents' home in Pocatello. Their number might have dwindled to three, but bless his stubborn heart, Matthew had not wanted to disappoint the remaining boys—Brian, Jason and Stephen Potter, the soccer coach's son.

Grace pulled into Matthew's circular gravel drive. The car had barely come to a complete stop before

Jason was out the door. She turned off the ignition. Matthew's wide porch was well lighted, but she didn't want to pull away until Jason was safely in the house.

The front door opened, and Matthew stepped outside. He motioned for Jason to go in, then closed the door behind him. Grace watched with foreboding as Matthew walked purposefully to her car. While he looked splendidly rugged in his jeans and long-sleeved hunter-green wool shirt, he didn't look like the bearer of good news. She fought back the urge to start her car and throw it into reverse.

When he stood beside her door, she rolled down the window slowly. "Problems?" she asked brightly, hoping he'd say no.

He bent down, his face just inches from hers. "Yeah."

"Oh."

"Stephen Potter's got the chicken pox."

"But he's already had it," protested Grace, vividly recalling the brigade of phoning mothers who'd reported their sons' measles, pox and mumps case histories to the school. She'd talked to Margaret Potter herself, and Stephen had already—

"Well, the kid's just made medical history because he's definitely sporting spots of the pox variety."

"You'll just have to reschedule the fishing, then. I'll run Jason back home." To bed, she added to herself.

"No. You're going fishing, Grace."

Since she'd been staring into Matthew's dark eyes, it took a moment for his words to sink in. By the time

they did, he already had her door open and was helping her out of her car. She looked down at the large
hand gripping her forearm. Helping? He was practically dragging her.

"There's no way I'm going fishing," she protested,
trying to dig the smooth heels of her sneakers into
the loose gravel drive. Neither her words nor her resistance slowed Matthew's progress. Absently she
concluded his ankle was fully recovered. "Let go of
me."

Abruptly he did, and Grace almost stumbled. She
caught her balance and pulled at the hem of the gray
sweatshirt that had ridden up to her midriff. Then she
smoothed her hair and squared her shoulders. Putting
herself to rights seemed crucial in gaining control of
the situation and giving Matthew the dressing-down
his outrageous behavior deserved.

"Now." She drew in a bracing gulp of morning
air. "It may have escaped your notice but I am *not* a
Webelo." She grabbed a fistful of her sagging sweatshirt. "See—no little blue uniform. I'm the mother of
a Webelo. *You're* the den leader. I sew on activity
badges—you help the boys earn them."

She smiled grimly. It was an arrangement that had
worked admirably in the past, and she had no intention of tampering with perfection.

Large hands settled gently on her shoulders. Grace
told herself she didn't feel a sudden lurch in the pit
of her stomach, a dozen dancing tingles or an inability
to catch her breath. And even if she did feel all that,
it was a well-known fact that skipping breakfast—

"Look, Grace, this is the chance we've been waiting for, the perfect opportunity to get the boys together in a relaxed atmosphere."

She decided that his definition of perfect and hers were two hundred miles apart. "So take them fishing, then. You don't need me. I don't know how to fish," she added for good measure.

"Neither do I."

Grace didn't feel a drop of pity at his chagrined expression. He had to be conning her. "But you're the den leader. You organized the stupid fishing activity in the first place."

"I know, but I figured at least half of the boys would be experienced enough to show the rest of us greenhorns what to do. Stephen Potter was my last hope. According to his dad, Stephen's fished ever since he's been out of diapers."

"Well, then, cancel the dumb activity. I want to go to bed." Grace saw the sudden glint in Matthew's eyes and flushed.

"I want to go to bed, too." His voice was low and gritty. "But I'm going fishing. And so are you. We're going down to the boat dock and spend a couple of hours with our sons—acting friendly and civilized. We'll drink some hot chocolate, drown a few of the worms Brian dug up last night and try to catch a damned fish. Two hours, Grace. That's all I ask."

Ask? Demand was more like it. She glanced away from Matthew's determined features and noticed that a pink dawn had begun to lighten the dark sky. Silhouettes of thick pines lining Matthew's property showed green now instead of black. Morning was fast approaching. If she were somehow magically transported back to her bed, she'd probably be unable to fall asleep again.

"All right, I'll stay."

"Good. Now come on—our sons have been alone in my house for almost ten minutes."

Grace tagged after Matthew, taking two steps to each of his giant ones. Looking back on their skirmish, she was a little astonished at the way she had stood up to Matthew. She'd never considered herself the least bit feisty.

She followed him to the porch and decided her militant mood had something to do with being awakened at 5:00 a.m. on a Saturday morning. She closed Matthew's front door behind her and resolved to start getting up earlier—every morning. There was something wonderfully exhilarating about going toe-to-toe with Matthew Hollister.

"Looks like they've already gone down to the river." Matthew grabbed four bright orange life jackets from the dozen or so piled in a nearby heap. He tossed one to her. "Put this on and meet me at the dock."

"Where is it?"

"Through the kitchen, out the side door and down the terrace. The gravel path leads straight there."

"Thanks." He had already left the room and was on his way to the river.

Grace eyed the tightly stuffed, slippery orange vest she held and wondered why she needed it. Despite what Matthew had said, she had no intention of being anything but a distant—very distant—spectator this morning.

She walked through Matthew's kitchen, noticing the large pot of bubbling hot chocolate on the stove. She stopped for a moment to survey the incredible mess surrounding the lone pot. Two emptied milk cartons—one on its side, a ripped sack of granulated sugar and a giant-size tin of cocoa with its lid off covered one countertop.

Another counter was littered with at least eight spoons, each one puddled with chocolate milk. A torn bag of fluffy marshmallows and assorted mugs added to the confusion. It was the milk-lined measuring cup and the cookbook covered with sugar and cocoa that brought a smile to her lips. She turned down the flame heating the simmering chocolate.

It would be a shame to scorch something Matthew had so obviously labored over. Grace gave the disaster site a final glance. Matthew's housekeeper might never take off another Saturday.

The gravel path curved through a grove of tall-masted pines. After three winding turns, she could see Matthew and the boys standing on the grass-covered bank above the bobbing, weathered platform that evidently was the dock. It was light enough for her to make out the boys' intent expressions as they concentrated on Matthew's words.

Beyond them the Snake River looked gray, cold and fast moving. Lethal. She shivered, grateful that

Matthew had planned ahead and invested in life jackets. She paused for a moment to slip into the one she'd carried from the house. Then she joined the trio of fishermen.

Brian was speaking. "I'll go get them, Dad."

"Okay. Jason and I will get the fishing rods ready." Matthew picked up a springy rod and flexed it a couple of times.

Grace couldn't help noticing the price tags dangling from both the narrow pole and its reel. Several other shiny new fishing rods leaned against a nearby lodge-pole pine. And the tackle box Jason was poking around in looked large enough to use as an anchor for the *Queen Mary*. It must have had more than a hundred miniature compartments—each one overflowing with metal lures, red-and-white bobbers, hooks and flat spools of nylon tackle.

"Did the salesman who sold you all this stuff work on commission?" She couldn't keep the amusement from her voice.

Matthew laid aside the rod he'd been fiddling with and reached for another. His smile might have been sheepish, but his eyes sparkled with masculine enthusiasm. "If you're going to do a good job, you need the proper tools."

Tools? Toys was more like it. She stepped closer and watched as Matthew threaded the nylon line through a small silver weight. "How come you look like you know what you're doing?"

Matthew looked up from his task. "Shh, you're going to blow my image." He nodded significantly toward Jason, who was looking in awe at a realistic dragonfly attached to a three-pronged hook.

"You do know what you're doing!" she challenged in a low-pitched voice.

"Usually when a good-looking woman tells me I know what I'm doing she's smiling."

Grace's mouth fell open. Was he flirting with her? She stared at him angrily. If he was, he'd picked the wrong time *and* the wrong woman on which to try his...his manly wiles.

"Matthew Hollister, you lied to me."

He leaned toward her and Grace jumped back, then flushed when she realized he was merely laying his fishing rod next to the others resting against the tree. "I didn't lie; the only thing I know about fishing is what I read in this brochure last night." He pulled a folded booklet from his back pocket and handed it to her.

"See—everything you ever wanted to know about fishing."

Grace skimmed the thin booklet and then handed it back to Matthew. "You seem to catch on awfully quick." She could feel her cheeks heat with color. Why was it he made her self-conscious of everything she said to him?

"I've been told I have an aptitude for—"

"Here, Dad," Brian interrupted. The boy held out two cups.

"Thanks, son. Hand them to Mrs. Banner for a minute while I help Jason set up his rod."

An aptitude for what? wondered Grace as she followed Matthew to Jason's side. Absently she raised one of the cups to her lips. Some hot chocolate would—

"Eeek!" Grace flung the crawling contents of the cup into the air.

A dozen fat worms rained down, most of them landing on the shirtfront of an astonished Matthew Hollister. "What the—"

"They're worms!" Grace cried, shuddering.

"Hell, yes, they're worms!" Matthew exclaimed in consternation as he began plucking the traumatized creatures from his shirt. "What'd you think they were?"

"Chocolate, hot chocolate," Grace said weakly, holding a trembling hand over her heart.

Matthew dropped the last worm into the cup Brian had retrieved for him. He stared at Grace first incredulously, then sympathetically. "In that case, we owe you a cup of—good Lord, I forgot about the cocoa. Brian, run back up to the house and turn off the stove before we start a fire."

Her heartbeat returning to something resembling normal, Grace spoke up. "I turned the burner down as I came through the kitchen. It should be all right."

"Thanks. I can't believe how tough it is to make that stuff. I didn't think I'd ever get those clumps of cocoa to dissolve." He turned to Jason. "Why don't you help Brian bring the mugs. We'll all have some. Then, sometime before noon, I swear we're going fishing."

When they were alone, Grace stared self-consciously at her sneakers. She felt more than a little foolish for trying to drink their bait.

"Come here, Grace."

She looked up and found herself trapped in Matthew's quiet stare. He extended a hand to her. She studied his large, callused palm for several seconds before slipping her fingers into his. He led her to a large, smooth rock.

"Sit with me; I think we both need to catch our breath."

The rock was wide enough to accommodate both of them—if they sat very close together. They did.

"Was there anything in your book about flying worms?"

The edges of Matthew's mouth quivered. Matthew's mouth… Grace rolled the phrase around in her head. It had a very provocative ring to it.

"I think that's covered in volume two." His burgeoning grin made the laugh lines fanning out from his eyes more prominent.

"I feel like such a greenhorn."

He chuckled. "Join the club."

When his arm settled companionably around her shoulders, she suddenly remembered she hadn't had breakfast. She remembered because of the lurch and skittering tingles in her stomach and her breathlessness.

"After a cup of cocoa, you'll feel more like fishing."

Neither Grace nor Matthew noticed the two solemn boys standing a few feet behind them on the gravel

path. They couldn't know how right they looked together. But Jason and Brian, watching, felt the right-
ness. They stared steadily at their parents for a long
moment, then turned and glanced meaningfully at
each other.

Surprisingly enough, Matthew was right. A cup of
hot chocolate had hit the spot. Grace stood with her
feet planted on the swaying dock and tilted her face
to the morning sun. Instead of a murky gray, the river
was now a frothy, sea-foam green. The wonderful,
fresh scent of pine permeated the air. And overhead
silver clouds drifted with regal sedateness against the
bold turquoise sky.

She returned her attention to the fishing pole that
rested laxly in her left hand. Neither the boys nor
Matthew had noticed it was only a prop with no living
organism impaled on its hook. She'd come as close
as she was going to get to the worm members of their
fishing party.

Thus far Matthew Hollister, novice and greenhorn
extraordinaire, had been the only one to catch anything. Accompanied by the excited shrieks of the
awed boys, he had landed three impressive rainbow
trout.

Brian was fishing off the same side of the small
dock as Grace. Jason's and Matthew's lines drifted
from the front of the platform. Every time Matthew
caught a fish, Jason or Brian would move to stand
where he had been.

"Hey! Hey, I got something!" Brian shouted suddenly.

"Grace, reel in so you don't get tangled in his line," Matthew instructed calmly.

Grace bit back a smile. Three lousy fish and he was Mr. Know-it-all. "Yes, sir."

"Easy, Brian. You've got him. Let him run a little. He'll tire. Then you can tighten your drag."

"He's a giant!" yelled a wide-eyed Jason.

"Hand me your pole, Jason, and get the net."

Jason scrambled across the dock and lunged for the net.

"That's it, Brian. He's coming. He's coming. Slow and easy. Let him go, it's all right. He wants to run some more. You've got him. You've got him. Jason, use the net! Now!"

Jason dipped the net into the river and pulled out a wriggling, dripping fish. "Man, oh, man, Brian. It's twice the size of what your dad caught!"

Brian gazed proudly at his monster fish, then at Jason. "Thanks, I couldn't have landed him without you."

Grace's and Matthew's gazes met. Operation Friendship was alive and thriving. Then the nearby hum of a jet boat drew their attention to the river. A sixteen-foot launch with two men in it motored past.

Matthew turned to Brian. "That is a beauty, son. Lay him on the bank next to mine. We're going to have a fish fry tonight that—" He broke off and glanced at Grace.

"You clean them and I'll cook them," she said in answer to the unspoken question in Matthew's eyes.

"Hey, Mom, your worm fell off your hook. You'll never catch anything that way. Here, let me bait it for you."

Grace watched philosophically as Jason attached a worm to the end of her line. "How much longer do you think we'll be out here?" The morning sun was getting stronger, and her sweatshirt had begun to feel overly warm.

"Until I catch something," Jason answered determinedly.

Luckily in the next few minutes Jason was able to hook a fish. It wasn't as large as Brian's, but it had fought a good fight. The flush of victory heated her son's proud features.

"I guess that does it, then," said Grace, beginning to reel in. Her eyes widened when her line took off in the opposite direction.

"Hey, Mom's got something!"

"Easy, Grace, don't reel in too quickly," came Matthew's immediate advice.

She held on to her rod and reel for dear life. "I know, I know."

The next seconds passed in a flurry of excited instructions from the boys and cool commands from Matthew. Her fish splashed, dipped, bobbed and jumped. He was a fighting demon. But she had no intention of letting him go. He was hers, and she was going to land him.

"Grab the net, Brian, grab the net!" shouted Jason. Grace grinned victoriously. "I got him!"

Matthew took one look at her beaming face and laughed. "I think he's got you. You caught the biggest damn fish of any of us."

"I did, didn't I?" She watched Brian and Jason work together to dislodge the hook from the fish's lower lip.

The four triumphant fishermen looked up when they heard the sound of a boat motoring to the dock. It was the jet boat that had passed by earlier. First one man, then another stepped gingerly onto the landing. Grace noticed the fifty-cent-size silver badges attached to their dark green Windbreakers, testifying that the men were Idaho fish-and-game wardens.

"Looks like you've been doing pretty good this morning," observed the taller of the pair.

"My mom caught this one." Jason held up the long German brown by its gill flaps.

"Quite a fish there, ma'am." He looked admiringly at the wet fish. "Too bad it's over the length of what you can keep. Better get it back into the water, son."

"I thought you threw fish back when they were too little," Grace protested.

"Used to be that way," responded the second man. He directed his attention to the rest of their catch. "Looks like your other fish are all within the legal limit."

There was a splash and Grace watched her fish float lifelessly for a moment before readapting to the water and taking off like a torpedo. It occurred to her that there was more pleasure in letting the fish go than there had been in catching it. Clearly she was not a born fisherman.

The taller agent cleared his throat. "May I see your licenses?"

"You bet," Matthew said. "Now, the boys are under twelve so they don't need them, right?"

The men nodded. Matthew stepped in front of Grace, edging her back on the dock. He reached beneath his life jacket and then extended a small white piece of paper to the wardens.

Suddenly it dawned on Grace that *she* didn't have any little piece of paper to present. She began to inch backward, her sneakered feet slowly carrying her from the talking men. She didn't get far.

The game warden examining the paper Matthew had given him looked up. "And you, Mrs. Hollister— may we see your license?"

She supposed it was a natural mistake for the officer to think she and Matthew were married. She could overlook that. She only hoped he'd be equally willing to overlook the small matter of her fishing without a license. She shot a furious glance at Matthew—the man who'd practically dragged her from her car and forced a pole into her hands. He was frowning.

"Well, actually..." she began, bringing her gaze back to the game warden. "I don't have a license." She smiled apologetically.

The warden didn't smile back. "That's too bad."

He reached inside his jacket and pulled out a pen and small pad.

When he flicked open the pad, Grace saw it was filled with tidy little carbon forms very similar to the kind the highway patrol used when writing tickets. She'd never had a traffic ticket in her life, but she'd ridden with drivers who'd been pulled over and cited.

Darn, her first ticket and it was for *fishing*. She speared Matthew with another hot glare. She ought to make him pay the fine. Then she looked at Jason. He was staring at her with huge eyes. No wonder. His mother was a felonious fisherman.

"Just for the record, Officer. I'm not married to that man."

The game warden glanced up from his pad. Grace flushed. She hadn't meant to sound so abrupt. "I mean I'm not Mrs. Hollister."

A grin seemed to hover on the officer's mouth. "I'll need your full name and current address, ma'am."

Grace gave him the information and when she finished, Matthew stepped forward.

"Officer, it's my fault she was fishing without a license. There was a last-minute change in plans with our scout pack, and I forgot she needed a permit." He turned to Grace. "Don't worry. I'll pay your fine."

"Do you know what the fine is?" inquired the second game warden politely.

Matthew shook his head.

The officer writing the ticket answered. "From

twenty-five to one thousand dollars." He ripped off the top sheet of the form and looked at Grace sympathetically. "The season ends the last day in October. If you plan to do any more fishing before then, I suggest you get yourself a license—it's a much better bargain than paying a fine."

Grace nodded.

The game warden regarded her kindly. "You're the principal at Peninsula Elementary, aren't you?"

Grace nodded again.

"I thought so. My son goes to your school. You know something like this could be awfully embarrassing for you. A lot of times the newspaper prints citations like this in their News of Record column."

Grace nodded for the third time. She was going to strangle Matthew Hollister—with his own blasted fishing line!

The officer handed her the ticket. "Of course, a warning ticket like this isn't recorded. Nor is there a fine. In the future just remember to get yourself a license before you go fishing. You have a good day, now."

The two officers returned to their boat and started its motor. Very shortly they were out of sight.

Matthew sighed heavily. "Whew, that's a relief."

The sound of his voice pushed Grace over the edge of her self-control. She turned on him angrily. "You listen to me, Mr. Matthew Hollister—"

"Now, Grace—" He backed toward the dock.

She followed, closing the distance between them. "I have never been so humiliated in my whole life!"

She waved the warning ticket under his nose. ''Of course *you* had a license.''

Matthew had backed up as far as he dared on the small dock. He stood with his hands on his hips, staring down at Grace's flushed face. He had no idea why he felt so damned good. The woman was ready to rip his heart out and use it for bait.

But the sunlight danced off her rich brown hair, and her gray eyes flashed with vitality. There wasn't a bit of makeup on her glowing face. He didn't think he'd ever seen such a beautiful woman. Somewhere near the region where his heart pumped, he felt a curious spreading warmth.

''Don't just stand there grinning at me, you big lug!'' She jabbed a rigid index finger at his life jacket. ''This could have been serious.''

Matthew fought the urge to press that angry little finger to his lips. ''I'm sorry, you have every reason to be mad at me,'' he said softly, his dark eyes shining.

All at once his apology made her feel small and petty. ''Well, just see that it doesn't happen again.'' She stared up at the sharp masculine angles of his face and felt her anger dissolve. Every muscle in her body seemed to relax.

He stared back at her. Both felt the dock bobbing beneath their feet, a cool breeze wafting gently across their flushed skin—and an irresistible force drawing them closer.

A moment passed, then two. It was Jason's yell that

brought Grace and Matthew back to earth with a thud. "Mom, your ticket's blowing away!"

With a start Grace realized she'd let the paper slip from her fingertips. The light wind had caught the ticket and whipped it above her head. She automatically jumped for it.

"Watch out!"

But Matthew's warning came too late.

The dock dipped sharply to one side. Matthew caught his balance, but, her attention focused on the airborne paper, Grace slipped and tumbled over the side of the dock and into the icy river.

Instantly Matthew's arm shot out and seized the collar of her life jacket. In less than a minute, he hauled her from the freezing water. She lay sprawled in a drenched, shivering heap at his feet.

"Grace, are you all right?" He bent down and swiftly loosened her life jacket.

"Ju-just pe-peachy." Her teeth were chattering so badly that she had to be careful to keep her tongue out of harm's way.

Matthew jerked off his dry wool shirt and wrapped it around her trembling form. He helped her to her feet, and with his arm about her shoulders, he led her toward the gravel path.

"Come on, honey. I'll take care of you."

Neither Grace nor Matthew noticed his husky endearment, but Brian and Jason did. And as they moved to gather up the poles and fishing equipment, their eyes met and held more than once.

Chapter Seven

Matthew's bedroom came as something of a surprise to Grace. Wrapped precariously in a thick royal-blue towel, she stood in the center of the spartan room. Matthew had taken the wet clothes she'd extended through the partially opened bathroom door, and right this moment said clothing was spinning around in his dryer.

Grace nibbled her lower lip. Recalling the obvious difficulty he'd encountered in trying to make hot chocolate, she could only hope he was more familiar with how to operate the dryer. She didn't look forward to having her clothes returned to her charbroiled.

Absently she readjusted the blue towel. She didn't want to think about him handling the undergarments she'd wrapped inside her jeans and sweatshirt. She could feel her skin heating with a blush. Why had she chosen today to wear the skimpy lace bra and panties?

Again she adjusted the towel that seemed more inclined to obey the law of gravity than any code of modesty. Necessity had demanded that her wet garments be dried and practicality had demanded that Matthew be responsible for the drying. She had no reason to feel embarrassed. Besides, Matthew Hollister had probably seen lots of women's lacy underthings in his life as a bachelor. He wouldn't bat an eye at attending to hers.

Grace hugged the towel tighter and turned slowly to study the bedroom. Matthew's bed was merely a functional double, instead of the king-size one she'd have assumed someone of his substantial frame would have felt comfortable in. The headboard was a slab of pale oak, and mocha-brown sheets lay twisted about the wheat-colored blankets and white spread. She stared at the rumpled bed for several minutes.

Light streamed into the room from floor-to-ceiling windows opening onto a terrace that overlooked a secluded, pine-fringed cove. The room's floor was hardwood, beautifully polished with a thick cream-colored throw rug beside the bed. The rest of the furnishings—a triple dresser, chest of drawers and two nightstands framing the bed—were made of smooth oak. Airy and bright, Matthew's bedroom smelled of lemon oil and an elusive combination of Idaho sunshine and citrusy after-shave.

Grace felt her gaze pulled again to Matthew's bed. Somehow she couldn't keep from seeing him in it. It was uncanny how vividly she could picture his muscular body wrapped in the dark sheets and pale blankets. No matter how she stretched her imagination, however, she couldn't visualize him in a conservative pair of pajamas. He didn't seem the kind of man who would sleep in anything save his skin.

Then she remembered what it had felt like to be pressed against his bare chest, a chest that was broad and hard and softly furred. Grace continued to stare moodily at his bed. It was odd how aware she was of a man she refused to be attracted to.

She tried to summon up her earlier anger at the compromising situation he'd put her in with the game wardens, but the anger wouldn't return. Instead she was overcome by a racing montage of the morning's events: Matthew's determined features when he demanded she fish with their sons, his expression of astonishment when she'd flung a dozen worms at him, the pure joy he'd radiated with a fighting trout on the end of his line.... He'd been so proud of Brian when he'd landed his German brown. And equally proud of Jason when he'd snagged a rainbow trout.

And his expression when the game wardens had showed up.... Grace couldn't keep from grinning. He'd been quaking in his tennis shoes.

A knock at the bedroom door scattered her thoughts in four different directions. "Grace, your things are dry."

She approached the door, hitching up the towel as she went. Again she thrust a bare arm through a partially opened door. Instead of the weight of her dried clothes, however, she continued to feel nothing but air.

Curious, she opened the bedroom door wider. Her gaze trailed up Matthew's chest, now covered in a red-and-blue plaid shirt, to a silken tuft of brown hair at his throat. She jerked her gaze beyond that strangely tantalizing sight to his dark eyes. Glittering eyes.

And the target of those glittering eyes was herself—wrapped only in the meager protection of a towel. She moved back, her naked arm still stretched toward him.

Matthew knew he had no damned business stepping into his bedroom and closing the door behind him. Yet he seemed unable to help himself. He focused on the slender perfection of the feminine arm reaching for the clothes he held. Beyond that pale, soft arm were delicate shoulders. He had to look at her, to study the gentle swell of the ivory skin of her breasts. One tug. One tug on the towel would grant him what he wanted to see.

But he made the mistake of looking into Grace's face before he claimed what he wanted. In her wide gray eyes, he read shock, fear—excitement? He honestly wasn't sure. He only knew with a sudden stomach-wrenching burst of sanity that this had been Blake's woman. She couldn't be his.

He retreated a step and put the neatly folded garments into her open palm. Her hand dropped under the sudden weight and her other one automatically came up to catch the falling clothes. The blue towel slipped open.

Matthew turned and jerked at the door. He strode through it, then slammed it soundly behind him. Too late.

"Gosh, Mrs. Banner, you sure are a good cook."

Grace looked up from the dishwasher she was loading with lunch dishes and smiled. "Thank you, Brian."

His spoon made a final journey into the bowl of homemade chicken noodle soup. It was the fourth helping he'd finished. Then his hand curled around his glass and he drained it of milk for the third time. When he sat the glass on the table, a milk mustache graced his young mouth.

She crossed the kitchen and handed him a napkin. With a quick swipe, he eradicated the mustache. "I sure wish you'd give Mrs. Humphrey your recipe. I know my dad would love those noodles."

Grace sighed. In the two weeks since their fishing adventure and the high drama in Matthew's bedroom, she'd seen Brian's father half a dozen times. Briefly. They had exchanged perhaps two dozen words. All superficial. She told herself that was for the best. The only reason she and Matthew saw each other in the first place was to implement his grand plan for Brian and Jason to spend time together so they could become friends. She also told herself that nothing, nothing at all had happened in Matthew's bedroom.

Her gaze lingered on Brian. In keeping with Matthew's strategy, Brian and Jason had spent a lot of afternoons together. There hadn't been any major fireworks. Both boys had performed the joint tasks

Matthew had assigned them. And yet there was a kind of shuttered attitude on the part of Brian and Jason that bothered Grace. She had the feeling something was happening beneath the surface of their feud that she couldn't quite figure out.

On this particular Saturday afternoon, Matthew had had to make a run to the county dump in his dad's pickup truck. He had suggested Jason take the ride with him instead of Brian. She couldn't help wondering what Matthew and her son would find to discuss.

"Thanks for lending me Jason's Webelos shirt. Mrs. Humphrey sewed on all the patches and stuff on mine."

"You're welcome."

"I can hardly wait until I earn all the pins and everything," Brian went on.

"It won't take you long. Jason earned all those awards in less than a year. At the rate your dad is going, you boys will be eligible for every activity badge there is."

Whatever Matthew's business problems might be, he'd found the time to have two meetings weekly with the Webelos. The boys were in seventh heaven with their new den leader. There had been more fishing adventures, campouts in backyards and all kinds of rope-tying sessions.

Brian scooted back his chair and joined Grace at the sink. "Whatcha doing?" His brown eyes studied the small apples she had began to peel and core.

"Making apple dumplings."

"I never heard of them. Are they good?"

"They're delicious." She smiled at the boy's hopeful expression. The way to this particular young man's heart was definitely through his stomach. "Why don't I make an extra dish of them for you to take home?"

"That would be great." He continued to watch as she packed the brown sugar and butter in the hollowed-out apple centers. "I bet I could do that."

"I bet you could at that. Want to try?"

He nodded enthusiastically, and for the next hour they worked side by side. After the apples had been put into the oven to bake, Brian followed Grace downstairs to the basement. He helped her retrieve a couple of boxes containing old stage and dance costumes Jason's grandparents had given her.

She noticed a colorful pirate outfit caught his eye and felt no qualms about lending it to him. There were a half dozen similar ones for Jason to choose from if he wanted to be a pirate on Halloween.

Matthew and Jason returned around five o'clock, and the mouthwatering aroma of cinnamon, brown sugar, bubbling apples and homemade pie crust permeated the air.

"Oh, Lord, you could bottle that smell, Grace, and rule the world."

Grace bit her bottom lip as she watched Matthew circle the steaming glass dish of dumplings. Like father, like son. If she ever wanted to seduce Matthew Hollister, rather than a peekaboo black lace teddy or even complete nudity, she'd have better luck with food. Grace's fingers went to her forehead as if to censor her unexpected X-rated thoughts. This was going to have to stop.

Matthew Hollister did *not* belong in her mind. There wasn't room enough for him there. Not room enough for him and her feeling of loyalty to Blake, at any rate.

"If the urge to rule becomes too much for me, I'll keep that in mind."

He shot her an amused glance.

And you, Matthew Hollister. If you ever decide to rule the world, all you need to do is bottle that earthy, virile energy you radiate.

He wore a deep red plaid shirt with faded jeans that accented his powerful thighs. His dark hair looked recently trimmed and his brown eyes were filled with warmth and contentment and affection. How did he manage to look so darned sexy?

His gaze had come to rest on the second dish of golden dumplings. "Can they possibly taste as good as they smell?"

Grace laughed. "Yes, Matthew, they can. And guess what? You get to find out for yourself how good they are. The second dish is for you to take home."

The spontaneous grin that lighted his rugged face awakened the overwhelming urge in Grace to kick Matthew Hollister in the seat of his pants. Would it be so terrible if he looked at her with that same kind of hungry anticipation? Mentally Grace shook herself.

Of course it would be terrible. It would be a major calamity.

"I don't know if I can wait until we get home."

"They're too hot to eat right now...." Grace's words slowly trailed away. Somehow, in the space of milliseconds, Matthew's hungry expression seemed to encompass...*her*. Breathing became a conscious act.

"Too hot to handle?" His voice was a husky murmur.

No, she was imagining things. Her hand went to her forehead again. Her wicked, carnal thoughts had overloaded her brain cells and she was hallucinating. Matthew really hadn't stepped closer to her. The angle of his bent head really hadn't placed his firm mouth a breath away.

"Ah, Grace, I—"

"Hey, Dad!" Brian's yell filled the small kitchen. Matthew and Grace sprang apart. "That movie comes on TV in fifteen minutes. We gotta go."

"Right." Matthew felt as if he'd just been plucked one step away from a pool of quicksand. So why wasn't he feeling relieved? Why was he feeling so damned frustrated?

"Don't forget your dumplings. Here's some hot pads."

I don't want your damned dumplings. I want you. And you I can handle without the hot pads. He backed away from her, one step at a time. She was a witch. She was a demon. She was...the most appealing, irresistible and desirable woman he'd ever known. But, he reminded himself, she was off limits. Off limits because… In that instant, for the life of him, he couldn't remember what had kept him from acknowledging and responding to Grace Banner's gentle allure.

An allure, he admitted to himself, that was stronger than mere physical attraction. There was an intangible something about her, a mysterious but nevertheless real quality of sweet intensity that pulled at him. He didn't want to belive it was her marriage to Blake that formed the basis of his fascination with her. But neither was he ready to believe her appeal sprang from anything else.

It was a full half hour after Matthew Hollister had left the premises before Grace's pulse rate returned to anything resembling normal. As she and Jason sat in the family room watching a drenched muskrat climb onto a river-tossed log in order to survive a raging flash flood, all she could think about was how Matthew had stared at her before Brian's call had shaken her kitchen rafters.

She'd bet next month's budget allotment that Matthew Hollister hadn't been thinking about her dumplings. Her fingers absently tapped the sofa's armrest. It was a good thing she wasn't a gambling woman. The school board wouldn't take kindly to her losing its money.

Darn it all. Matthew Hollister was sexier than any mortal man had a right to be. And he'd come tearing into her life, making her feel all sorts of warm—no, *hot*—and tingly feelings that she was better off not feeling. The plain and simple fact was—he tempted her. Tempted her to forget that he had been Blake's foe, that their sons hated each other and that since his wife's death, Matthew Hollister, it appeared, was no longer the marrying kind.

Grace had no doubt Matthew had tempted many women during the past nine years. How many of them had yielded to that temptation, and where were they now? Out of his life after a brief fling? For some reason Enid Coulson's image popped into Grace's mind. Yes, even the militant social worker would find herself tempted by Matthew Hollister. Oh, she might decide he needed to be whipped into shape before he met her exacting standards, but even she would melt at his feet. The size of the resulting puddle made Grace giggle.

"Mom, this isn't funny. Those wolves might have Tango for breakfast."

Grace's gaze went to the TV screen where the bedraggled muskrat was now encircled by five growling, ferocious wolves dripping saliva. She shuddered. "I guess not."

Miraculously, in two action-packed minutes, Tango did escape the marauding band of hungry wolves. Unfortunately a black bear skulking through the forest made any sense of relief premature.

"Jason, there aren't any wild animals where you and the Webelos camp, are there?"

"There sure are." The boyish satisfaction in his voice was daunting.

"When you say 'wild,' you don't mean—"

"Shh, Mom. I think that bear is hungrier than that pack of wolves was."

"Come on, Mom. I signed you up from seven to eight."

Grace lengthened her stride to keep up with Jason as he weaved his way through the noisy, tightly packed gym. Among the other vivid Halloween costumes worn by the children and adults in attendance, his bright green satin shirt and black britches were not easy to keep track of.

She'd allowed Jason to sign her up to work in one of the carnival booths, and she still didn't know which one he'd chosen or what other parent would be helping her run it. He moved swiftly past the fishing pond, cake walk and fortune-teller. Then he stopped in front of the dart-throwing booth. Two smiling but harried-looking mothers cheered Grace's arrival.

"Reinforcements!"

"Reinforcements, heck. Mrs. Banner is our relief. You and I are out of here, Illa Mae."

Grace laughed good-naturedly, taking her place inside the cramped booth. "That rough, hmm?"

"The kids are great," countered Illa Mae, wiping her perspiring brow with the long sleeve of her pioneer costume. "It's just there's so *many* of them."

Smiling philosophically, Grace accepted a handful of colorful darts. Then a husky, devastatingly familiar voice brought a quick demise to her smile.

"Don't worry, Grace and I can handle the situation."

Don't bet on it, thought Grace when she turned and faced the sexiest pirate she'd ever seen. Of course, her life being what it was, she hadn't had any contact with a flesh-and-blood pirate. In fact her only experiences had been via the printed page. But those encounters had been…heated.

Dressed in a loose-fitting red silk shirt and snug black trousers, Matthew Hollister looked every inch the devilish buccaneer. A black eye patch further enhanced his rakish appeal. Her eyes focused on the gold earring adorning one tanned earlobe. She swallowed. Somehow the simple decoration seemed very provocative.

It required little imagination to picture him as a real wielder of swords. And had he and she lived in an earlier time, Grace realized she would have been very susceptible to his primitive allure.

"Grace?"

"Hmm?"

"This dart game would be more exciting for the children if we provided them with darts," observed Matthew mildly, his unobstructed eye regarding her with mesmerizing intensity.

Grace forced herself to concentrate on the colorful darts she clutched. "I know that."

Hurriedly she moved to the front of the line of miniature monsters, superheroes and fanciful cartoon creatures and handed a waiting gypsy princess the three darts her ticket entitled her to. Then, she stepped aside to allow the girl an unimpeded right-of-way to the cluster of balloons taped to a large sheet of plywood.

She bumped into Matthew. "Excuse me." Inwardly she commanded herself to get a grip on her fantasies and ignore the tremors skittering through her. There was one thing for darned sure. She had absolutely read her *last* historical romance. Well, the last one featuring hunklike pirates, anyway.

Grace flashed Matthew a quick glance. His complacent smile grated on her nerves. When green and blue balloons popped loudly in quick succession, she jumped. Then she forced her stiff lips to assume a beaming smile, which she directed to the little gypsy.

"Two out of three. Super job." She reached into a large box, fished out an oversized pair of red sunglasses and handed them to the wide-eyed girl.

"Gee, thanks!"

"Quite a coincidence, hmm?" inquired Matthew quietly, attaching more inflated balloons to the plywood.

Grace's head jerked around. "You mean both of us working at the same booth?"

He shook his head. "No coincidence there; I'd say our sons set us up. I was referring to you and me and Jason and Brian all dressed as pirates." His gaze flowed warmly over her. "Of the four of us, I think you do the most for your costume."

Grace bent to retrieve a wildly tossed dart, and Matthew stooped to reclaim it at the same time. Grace found herself staring into the stark features of a roguish pirate. His hand enfolded hers, and for one wild moment out of time, she thought he was going to lean forward and kiss her. Instead he slowly helped her to her feet.

More balloons popped, breaking the tension between them. Without speaking, she accepted the darts Matthew pulled from the plywood board and then turned to a red-haired Indian maiden. She noticed her hand trembled when she handed the darts to the girl.

The following hour in the cramped booth was the longest of Grace's life. Time and again she would glance up to find Matthew staring at her. With the eye patch covering one eye, his gaze seemed strangely mysterious. What were his thoughts? And when the narrow confines of the booth forced them to brush against each other, what were his thoughts then?

"Looks like our replacements have arrived," observed Matthew quietly.

Grace started. "And I survived," she murmured softly.

"What?"

Grace turned to Matthew. "Uh, the time went by fast, didn't it?" She brushed against his solid frame twice more in trying to maneuver herself from the booth.

Grace was just drawing her first calm breath since seeing Matthew when she realized he'd followed her to the only visible square patch of floor space not filled with noisy, laughing people.

"Banner's Point hasn't forgotten how to throw a party."

Grace looked up into Matthew's strong face, then

glanced away. She was finding his powerful effect on her senses to be cumulative. It was then that she noticed for the first time the attention they were drawing from the other adults in the gym. It occurred to her that many of the people present were not comfortable with Blake's widow talking quietly to Matthew Hollister.

"I'm having a great time," continued Matthew.

"I—I'm glad."

"I especially like the idea of grown-ups wearing costumes. Yours is very appealing, Grace." His right hand reached out, and tanned, lean fingers gently brushed the silky fabric of her sleeve.

His husky voice slithered through her body like heated rum, while the warm pressure of his fingertips spoke directly to her feminine core. Grace blinked. She'd never even tasted rum—heated or otherwise, and the outside of his body had no business having an intimate discussion with the inside of hers.

"Th-thank you."

"Aren't you going to compliment me on mine?"

In her bemused frame of mind, his words made no sense. "Your what?"

He tipped his head forward and chuckled. "Oh, Grace, there's a dozen things I'd like to hear you compliment me on, but tonight I'll settle for you admiring my costume. Until Brian talked me into it, I wasn't going to wear one. It was nice of you to lend him one of Jason's."

When Grace finally made sense of Matthew's words, she flushed. "Jason's grandmother used to be

involved with the civic drama group. A few years ago
they did *The Pirates of Penzance*.''

''I see.''

Did he? she wondered. Did he see how strongly his
presence affected her? Somehow she doubted it.
Gamely Grace struggled to find a way to smoothly
dismiss him. She needed to regroup her emotions.
Something was happening between herself and this
man, something that she had to understand before she
let it overwhelm her.

When he was around, she became incredibly aware
of her femininity and her loneliness. Yet she'd never
been lonely until Matthew had slid out from beneath
the car he'd been working on the fateful day they'd
met. Since that day, she couldn't deny that in his presence, she felt more vitally alive, more complete than
she did alone.

Grace looked around the gym, desperately seeking
a socially acceptable means of putting some distance
between herself and Matthew. Her gaze halted when
she found one.

''I can't believe how thirsty I am....'' She let her
words trail off and looked longingly toward the punch
table.

Matthew's lips thinned, but he rose to Grace's gam-
bit. ''I'll get us some punch. Don't move,'' he added
as an afterthought before turning his back on her and
heading for the punch table.

''Don't move.'' Matthew grimaced. What a stupid
thing for him to say. But then he'd been feeling stupid
all night. What on earth was wrong with him? He'd

already decided weeks ago that nothing personal could develop between him and Grace Banner. Case closed. Finished. Period. Terminado!

So why was she always on his mind? Why did he find himself remembering how lovely she looked with the reflection of stained glass flickering over her delicate features? Or how she looked with sunshine splashing about her? Why was he so moved by how gently and carefully she considered Brian's and Jason's feelings each time she dealt with them?

And why was he so conscious of her sensuously curved body? Her soft, delectable and... His mind searched for the elusive, all-encompassing word that could explain what her body did to his. He searched in vain. All he knew was that the mere act of watching Grace Banner had fired an ache inside him that could only be eased by his becoming a part of her. He could feel the sweat on his brow as he remembered watching her bend over and reach into the prize box. Good Lord, he was becoming obsessed.

And his demented mind had been filled the entire night with her. With how the bright gym lights made the lighter strands of her dark brown hair gleam with golden highlights. With how her wide gray eyes regarded him half fearfully, half... What had he seen in her eyes tonight? The counterpart to his own sudden desire?

Grace watched Matthew fill two clear plastic glasses with crimson punch and continued drawing slow, steady breaths. She'd never hyperventilated in her life and she wasn't about to start now. The evening was almost over. Surely she was mature enough to engage in a few more moments of civilized chitchat with Matthew Hollister.

Her mental pep talk worked until she made the mistake of allowing her gaze to return to Matthew. He was walking back carrying two glasses of punch. Each step he took seemed to radiate hard, primitive vitality. Her mind became filled with half-formed images of midnight trysts, whispered endearments and heady passions.

Shaken at her tangled thoughts, Grace stared at the tumbler of punch he extended as if it were poison and the large hand supporting it a lethal hook. How had this man gained so much power over her emotions?

Slowly Grace moved her gaze across his arm, past a broad shoulder and up the corded column of his throat to finally encounter the riveting face of the man who'd stolen her sanity. At that moment all she wanted was to escape his confusing presence.

"I've changed my mind; I'm not thirsty after all." She spoke in a shaky whisper, spun around and marched straight into her son and his.

"Hi, Mom. Boy, this is sure a neat carnival. Did you see Stephen's costume? He came as a giant fly. Radical, huh?"

Grace's fingertips went to her forehead. "A fly? Well, yes, I guess that is pretty radical."

She noticed Brian melting away from Jason's side and her curious gaze followed him as he joined his father. The unwavering focus of Matthew's intense stare snared her for a full five seconds before she was able to free herself from it and meet her son's excited expression.

"It looks like you and Brian have finally decided to become friends," she suggested on a hopeful note, wanting to salvage some bit of encouraging news from the evening.

Jason flushed, then hedged. "Maybe."

"Maybe?"

"Well, he has something I want, and I have something he wants. We decided to share."

"Oh."

"Hey, you haven't been through the spook alley yet, have you?"

Despite her low spirits, Grace laughed. "I really hadn't planned on—"

"But you gotta! It's fantastic. It's more than fantastic. It's radical. It's, it's—"

"Awesome?"

"Right. Come on, Mom. You're going to love it."

Grace allowed herself to be led from the gym. Had she spared a backward glance, she would have seen Brian Hollister giving his father an identical rendering of Jason's energetic sales pitch.

Jason pushed open the side doors to the gym and took her hand. The corridor they entered had been darkened, and when the doors closed behind them, they were engulfed in total blackness.

As they walked, Grace mentally replayed her inexcusable rudeness to Matthew Hollister. Oh, dear, what had she been thinking? She sighed. That was just the point. She hadn't been thinking—not rationally, at any rate.

Following Jason's lead, they turned down a hallway leading toward the kindergarten classrooms. There must have been a last minute change of plans. Originally the spook alley had been planned for the end of the main corridor. She was about to ask Jason if he was sure of his direction when he stopped.

"You've got to go the rest of the way alone," he said in a sinister whisper.

In the darkness, Grace smiled. "Will I live to tell about my ordeal?" she whispered back.

She received no answer. Instead she heard the faint but distinct sound of a door being opened. The next thing she knew a pair of small hands were pushing her forward. Then the door slammed shut.

Grace knew two facts about her unexpected surroundings. She was in total blackness, and she was inside a broom closet. More specifically, she was inside the small broom closet located next to Mrs. Steltzer's kindergarten classroom. As she felt around the small closet with her hands, she discovered a third fact. She was alone.

This was certainly a new twist to their usual spook alley. Good-naturedly Grace settled back and awaited the closet's next occupant. She had no doubt it would be a chain-rattling ghost.

Only a minute passed before Grace heard the door to the small closet being opened again. She grinned. This might be fun, after all.

The door was quickly slammed shut, and Grace

sensed the arrival of another person or, if she was
guessing correctly, a ghostie. In the thick darkness,
she could hear the sounds of her new companion's
steady breathing. Calmly she waited for the terrifying
creature to make its vile presence known.

"I guess you got me. I surrender."

The deep masculine voice assaulted Grace's composure with the force of a drawn sword. Matthew
Hollister! She pressed her back against the closet wall
and practiced being invisible. When she found Jason,
she was going to—

"Come on, little goblin, I'm all yours. Do your
worst to me." His warm laughter bounced off the
closet walls, and she heard him moving around in the
narrow space that confined them.

She felt his exploring hand on her shoulder. It
moved to her arm, then paused for a moment. When
it moved again, she could feel him fingering the silky
material of her blouse. Silence and darkness held
them both.

"Grace?"

Chapter Eight

Grace let out the breath she'd sucked into her lungs. There was no point in denying the obvious.

"Yes, it's me." Oh, why couldn't he have been a nice cooperative little ghostie?

Silence for a moment. "I suppose it's too much to hope that you arranged this...encounter."

Even through Grace's nervousness she could hear the wistfulness in his question. "I'm in this closet because my darling son lured me here."

"Oh."

"I suppose Brian engineered your arrival."

More silence.

"Ah, Matthew, are you still here?" She knew he was. She could still hear the sound of his breathing. Only now the breaths he drew seemed deeper and closer together.

"Yeah."

Husky and ragged, the word vibrated alarmingly close to her eardrum. He had moved nearer. She swallowed and reminded herself that, despite the pervasive darkness that embraced them, nearby crowds of people were laughing and enjoying themselves. What would they think if they knew Blake Banner's widow was carrying on in a dark closet with Matthew Hollister?

"Try the door; maybe it's not locked," she suggested in a thin voice.

She heard him twist the knob, but apparently nothing happened. To *it*. However when Matthew pressed his mouth close to her ear, an alarming thing happened to her pulse rate. It doubled, then quadrupled. Suddenly she felt as if there wasn't enough oxygen in the entire world, let alone in this tiny closet, to supply her lungs with breath.

"They've locked us in," he announced with seeming disregard for the primitive forces raging through her trembling body.

She wanted to tell him to take his mouth away from her ear, but she seriously doubted she could do so without betraying her shameless reaction to his close proximity.

And shameless was how Grace felt. She found herself wishing Matthew Hollister really were a pirate, one who would seize the moment—and her too. A kiss, oh yes, a kiss would have definitely been in order if—

She felt powerful hands grip her shoulders. "Dammit, Grace, I don't care if this is a mistake."

His firm mouth found hers in the darkness, and his hard chest pressed against her swiftly racing heart. Hips and thighs met and joined, only the tissue-thin barriers of silk and satin keeping that joining from completeness. His large hands slipped to her bottom, gently cupping, and his hot, urgent mouth moved with stunning thoroughness to bind them. For now it was enough. It was everything.

Grace's fingers climbed to his shoulders, then to the back of his neck where her fingertips sank into a lush carpet of thick hair. He smelled of after-shave and tasted faintly of mint and tart punch. And, he felt… Oh, he felt hard and strong and wonderful.

The warm liquid heat his embrace aroused in her turned to fire, white-hot and blistering. She was glad the city code prevented storing combustible chemicals in closets. Between them, they were generating enough heat to ignite a fire storm that could reduce the entire building to a smoldering heap of ashes.

"Grace. Grace. Grace." His raspy voice was a litany of desire.

And, despite the fiery inferno inside her, Grace shivered. "Oh, Matthew." His name became an endearment.

His hot mouth had dropped to her throat. "You taste so damned good. And you feel…"

"Yes?" She wanted to hear the words.

"Wonderful. Perfect."

"So do you," she confessed softly.

He pulled her more tightly against him, and nothing of his manly need was left to her imagination. In the darkness, she felt him shift his stance, making a place for her between his powerful thighs.

Several dizzying minutes raced by. Then his shoulder brushed against an unseen object that rested against the closet wall, and a loud crash followed. ''Oh, Grace, why couldn't our sons have shut us up in a bedroom instead of this blasted closet?''

It took a moment before his hoarsely uttered complaint penetrated her passion-numbed brain. Then his earlier words came rushing back to her. He had called what they were doing a mistake. She refused to be a ''mistake'' in any man's life.

Grace felt his hands at the waistband of her slacks. He was untucking her blouse. What had moments before been blazing passion now became cold disillusionment. She began to struggle.

The primitive force of Matthew's hunger blinded him to Grace's sudden resistance and he continued to kiss and touch her at will. She tore her lips from his fiercely seeking mouth.

''No. Stop. Please stop.''

In the darkness, she felt him go suddenly still. His hands dropped from her waist and his mouth slowly ceased its hungry invasion of her tender lips. Moist heat imprinted the area he had possessed moments before.

''Why?'' The word was stark and cold, almost deadly in its precision.

Grace trembled. Matthew's furious anger was a living force within the small closet. She knew what men thought of women who played cruel games with their passions, and her skin burned in embarrassment. Then she squared her shoulders. She was under no obligation to consider the feelings of a man who could call this magical moment a mistake.

"You said it yourself."

"*I* said it?" Dark irony infused his words.

Grace heard him fumbling about in the darkness. There was another small crash and then a low curse from Matthew.

"What are you doing?" she asked suspiciously.

His answer came in a blinding flash of light as he flicked on the overhead bulb. She blinked owlishly. Now why hadn't she thought of that?

"Grace, you just interrupted the best necking session of my entire life. I'd like a better explanation than some incomprehensible statement that something I said turned you off!"

"Don't you dare yell at me."

"Grace..." His anger seemed to have faded and bemused frustration stamped his rugged features. "Does this have anything to do with you stalking out of the gym and leaving me holding two glasses of punch?"

She flushed and then nodded. "I'm sorry about that."

"Don't be sorry. Just tell me what's going on in that beautiful head of yours. I don't want there to be any misunderstandings between us, Grace." He radiated quiet sincerity.

"There's no misunderstanding. I understand perfectly. And so do you."

His sincere expression began to fray around the edges. "Fill me in, anyway."

The way Grace looked at it, she didn't have much choice in the matter. Being locked in a closet with the man significantly narrowed her options.

"It's all right, Matthew. I know you just..." Her words dwindled under his intense stare. Good grief, it certainly wasn't easy to tell a man face-to-face that she understood he'd gotten turned on and had lost his self-control with a woman with whom he had no intention of becoming serious.

"You realize, I just *what*?" he pressed determinedly.

"This would be easier for me if you turned off the light."

"The light goes out for serious necking and nothing else," he countered.

She couldn't tell whether he was joking and decided not to take the chance he might be. "Let me put it this way—I don't neck just for the fun of it."

Silent laughter claimed his features and Grace regretted her choice of words. Nevertheless, she raised her chin and stood by her explanation.

"Hmm. So I've got a 'serious' necker on my hands." His husky voice shook with humor.

Grace refused to let his amusement sidetrack her. How could it when she felt like crying?

"Matthew," she began again with soft intent. "I know encounters like this are different for men than they are for women. And I know it's easy to lose one's, er, self-control. But I don't take making love lightly. My *feelings* need to be involved, and I have pretty strong feelings. For me, something like what happened between us has to be more than just fun and games. It has to mean something. Do you understand?''

Any earlier amusement Matthew had felt vanished when Grace's words struck him. Raw hurt harshened his features. ''I'm beginning to. You don't fool around, right? You have to care for a man to be on intimate terms with him. Correct me if I'm not getting the point.'' He broke off and took a ragged breath.

She nodded, hoping he would say that what had happened between them had been more than a simple loss of his self-control.

''And I don't fit the bill, right?'' His hoarse question caught her completely off guard.

''*You* don't fill the bill?'' she asked incredulously.

He heard no question, only the bald statement that he could never be more to her than a romp in a closet.

''Well, I'm glad we got that cleared up.'' His hand gripped the doorknob.

Grace watched in amazement as the knob turned easily. ''The door wasn't locked?''

''No.''

''But you said—''

He cut her off. ''I figured our sons were trying their hands at matchmaking. Why disappoint them? You're a damned good-looking woman, Grace.'' His hot gaze fell to her body. ''And you've got a body that won't quit.'' His hard eyes returned to her face. ''I wanted it. A lot.''

"Just the body?" A crushing feeling of shame washed over her.

"No, not just the body—" Matthew broke off before he could admit he wanted all of her. Her mind. Her spirit. Her heart.... There was no way, however, he would confess his growing feelings for her when she'd just told him in no uncertain terms to take a hike!

Grace waited for Matthew to continue, wishing futilely that they could meet again as strangers. Strangers with no common past between them. Then she remembered. Even as a stranger, Matthew would be a widower and apparently unable to again commit himself to one woman, one love.

Matthew's harsh voice jerked her back to her surroundings, and his angry words splintered her wishes into nothingness.

"But, I would have *settled* for the body—to feel myself inside it, and you. Thanks for explaining why that's not going to happen—not in a damned closet, not in a bedroom, not in a million years."

He was gone before she could summon a response. It didn't matter, she thought disconsolately. She'd had no idea what she would have said to him. Her hand went to the light switch and once more the closet was pitched in blackness.

She retraced her steps toward the gym, stopping for a moment to pull herself together. But it took longer than a moment, much longer.

Grace's gaze went to the large round clock above the office file cabinets. Two o'clock, and all was well.

She dropped her pen on the stack of teacher evaluation forms she'd been filling out and massaged her temples.

All was *not* well. During the days that had elapsed since the Halloween Carnival, she had felt as if she were carrying an unwelcome burden on her shoulders. The burden of her and Matthew's shared anger. Only now the anger had left her, filtering out of her system in a steady stream of quiet despair.

She pushed back her chair and stood. All at once, the well-worn and familiar office that had served her for the past six years seemed to close in on her. The recess buzzer rang, and she moved to the windows that overlooked the school's front yard where a temporary playground had been improvised.

Squealing boys and girls scattered across the brittle, yellowed grass that housed their three pieces of playground equipment. As always, the race was to the swiftest, and the older boys and girls claimed the monkey bars and swings.

Grace tried to suppress the feeling of discouragement that washed through her as she watched the younger children contenting themselves with games of tag. Even dividing the older grades from the younger ones and holding separate recesses didn't solve the problem. But at least next year there would be ample space for the new playground equipment they'd been saving for.

She heard the low, vibrating rumble that announced the school's ancient furnace was kicking on and rubbed her palms against the silk sleeves of her pale green blouse. Unexpectedly the friction she generated filled her mind with the image of a rakish pirate. And as she'd done countless times the past week, she forced away the disturbing image and tried to focus on something else.

The scene outside her office window served as a handy diversion. The teachers on playground duty were tossing out soccer balls in order to lure the larger boys and girls from the swings. Grace watched as impromptu games flourished. The children were bundled up in coats and caps and mittens to protect them against the progressively colder days.

Then Grace's gaze was drawn to a blue pickup truck that drove slowly by the schoolyard and came to a stop across the street. The pickup's door opened and the short, familiar shape of Randolph Henshaw came into view. He strode toward the hand-painted For Sale by Owner sign that sat squarely in the center of his lot, hung a smaller sign over it, then stepped back. With sinking spirits, Grace read the boldly stenciled Sold sign. Well, that was that.

Loud, excited shouts from the children brought her gaze back to the playground where fat, lazy snowflakes had begun to drift downward from the grayish sky. Pandemonium reigned as laughing, shrieking children danced across the yard. The weatherman had forecasted a heavy snowfall, and Grace knew that by tomorrow morning the population of Banner's Point would be increased by the addition of a couple of hundred snowmen.

Resolutely Grace returned to her desk. Her busy schedule could not accommodate temporary time-outs for reflections on snowmen—or pirates. When she set aside the stack of papers two hours later, scarcely a minute passed before the secretary's voice came over the intercom, announcing she was locking up and calling it a day.

"Will you be working late again tonight, Mrs. Banner?"

"No, not tonight, Bonnie."

"That's good. I think we've got a major snowstorm brewing. Thank goodness it's Friday."

"It is Friday, isn't it?" asked Grace, only half kidding that she didn't know what day of the week it was.

"It is—and only two weeks until Thanksgiving vacation."

"That means we'll be stepping up the rehearsals for the Thanksgiving program."

"The slips with the children's parts in the program went out today."

"Do you think the Point is ready for a repeat of the landing on Plymouth Rock?" asked Grace, visualizing their small auditorium stage packed with pint-size Pilgrims and Indians.

"I'm sure we'll survive another year," Bonnie said with a laugh. "See you Monday."

Grace placed an elbow on her desk and rested her chin on the heel of her palm. Funny how when everything got quiet her thoughts persisted in returning to Matthew Hollister. She seemed to carry his craggy features around with her wherever she went. If only her last memory of him wasn't as he had been Friday night—embittered and angry.

Again and again she'd replayed in her mind their disastrous encounter in the broom closet. At each repetition she realized that she had been an equal partner in what had happened between herself and Matthew. That rankled. As a responsible adult, she had no right to blame him for losing his control.

Strength, tenderness, hunger—Matthew possessed all three in abundance. And for a few magic moments, his mouth had bound hers with fierce intensity. The hardness of his body, the cadence of his heartbeat, the scent and taste of him… In his desperate need, Matthew's desire for her had seemed to transcend the civilized restraints that separated modern man from his primitive forebears. But not once had his touch turned rough.

No, in passion Matthew Hollister was not a rough man. Though demanding, his mouth hadn't once bruised. The tenderness left Grace's eyes. But in his anger, he had been fearsome. Grace pushed back her chair and stood. Did she have the courage to face Matthew and explain what had made her draw away from him?

She knew his anger had been justified. She'd had no business giving him a lecture on…on morality, for heaven's sake. The man had only been kissing her, and she had practically accused him of being a sex fiend.

She reached for the gray wool jacket draped over

the back of her chair. Of course, there were kisses and then there were *kisses*. Matthew Hollister had a way of sweeping aside formalities like the clothes on their backs and the little matter of commitment.

She slipped into the jacket and reached for her purse. Commitment? He hadn't remarried in nine years. Commitment probably wasn't even in his vocabulary. And even if he should come to want more than a temporary affair with her, how could she be sure he wanted her for herself and not because he was still locked in his old rivalry against Blake?

Just the other night she'd been looking through Blake's high school senior yearbook with Jason. She had been stunned to see just how many times Matthew and Blake had competed against each other. Maybe Matthew's need to best Blake had filtered so deeply into his subconscious that even *he* didn't realize it was still a factor in his life.

Grace flicked off her office light and stepped into the hall. She didn't think she could bear it if she learned Matthew wanted her as some kind of battle trophy. Of course at this point her bout of self-questioning was academic. Matthew was probably so disgusted with her that he'd never speak to her again. Let alone kiss her.

"Damn."

As she walked down the corridor, Grace's heels clicked audibly against the green linoleum floor. Her depression at realizing that having Matthew kiss the living daylights out of her was a onetime occurrence made her forget for a moment that she *never* swore.

* * *

Grace decided that folding clothes was a lot like exploring outer space. You never reached the end of it. She had cooked and served dinner, which had consisted of pork chops, boiled potatoes and applesauce. The dishes were washed, the house tidied. Jason had gone to bed an hour ago. And the only thing separating her from a similar fate was a lumpy three-foot-tall, pyramid of laundry. It seemed she could keep up with every other aspect of housework save this one.

How on earth could a family of two go through so many clothes? The chime of her doorbell saved her from having to come up with the answer to that question and presented her with another. Who was paying her a visit at ten o'clock at night?

Her fingers went to the top button of her pink satin nightshirt and she fastened it. The nightshirt was short, hitting her several inches above her knees, but its tailored collar and short sleeves made it a fairly modest garment.

Grace headed for the living room, turning on lights as she went. She paused before her front door.

"Who is it?" In this day and age living in even a small town demanded routine precautions.

"Matthew Hollister."

Then again, there were always people and events for whom no precautions could be taken. Grace's fingers trembled as she unlocked the door and opened it. There indeed stood Matthew Hollister—lean, tall and covered with a layer of fluffy snow. For a crazy instant she realized that pirates and snowmen could be one and the same.

"Will you talk to me?" Grim determination marked his rough-cut features.

She nodded and stepped aside. A blustery draft of cold air followed him into the living room. It took Grace a moment to realize she hadn't closed the door. Red-faced, she hurriedly slammed it shut. The subsequent silence was deafening in its totality. It took a surprising amount of courage for her to turn and face Matthew. His expression was both serious and watchful.

"May I take your coat?" Was that cool, controlled voice hers? Grace shook her head in bewilderment at the strange games social propriety demanded when one's pride was on the line.

"Sure." He unbuttoned the heavy plaid coat and gazed surreptitiously at Grace. At first glance he thought she was attired in a perfectly proper nightgown that revealed no suggestive parts of her delectable anatomy.

He gritted his teeth. It was the second glance and his imagination that turned his insides to hot coals. For he realized that it was only his self-control, a distance of a few feet and a flimsy layer of pink satin that stood between himself and ecstasy.

The light streaming from the room's lamp cast Grace's entire body in highlights and shadows. Lighter strands of chestnut hair seemed to catch and reflect the light, while her face remained shadowed. The tips of her breasts became flashpoints, the tempting juncture of her thighs bathed in mysterious shadow. He swallowed. Hard.

Without speaking, he handed her his coat, making sure their hands didn't touch. He'd come here tonight to talk to her, not pull her into his arms.

"It's chilly in here. I was in the family room when you rang the doorbell. It's warmer in there." She knew she was babbling, but she had to do something to lessen the throbbing tension that stretched between them.

"Lead the way," he growled softly.

She turned, realizing suddenly that she was barefoot. All at once, she felt the overwhelming compulsion to excuse herself, flee to her bedroom and put her slippers on. Which of course was ridiculous since there was absolutely nothing suggestive about bare feet. Grace shook her head again in frustration. There was no doubt about it. Matthew Hollister was becoming a real threat to her sanity.

Matthew's dark eyes followed Grace's softly curved body with unwavering intensity. Highlight and shadow. The supple line of her spine, the narrow curve of her waist and the feminine swell of her hips ravaged his determination to communicate with her tonight only through the intimacy of words. They needed the words. He was convinced the other intimacies would come. But there could be no physical surrender to the attraction sizzling between them until the words had set them free.

Midway into her family room, Grace came to an abrupt halt. In her surprise at seeing Matthew on her doorstep, she'd forgotten what she'd been doing before his arrival. Somehow the stacks of neatly folded underclothes that cluttered her couch seemed a personal extension of herself—like her bare feet. And his volatile presence inches away from her silky slips, lacy bras and skimpy panties was a disturbing invasion. Haphazardly she began scooping up the clothes. "I'll just set these aside."

Matthew's thoughts were on matters other than lingerie. Since entering the room, he had literally been unable to tear his gaze from Grace. When she bent over to retrieve the garments, he blanched. The hem of her pink nightshirt crept dangerously high, and his fingers went to the suddenly too-tight collar of his shirt. She had been right about one thing. It was a helluva lot hotter in here than in the living room.

Grace turned and smiled shyly at Matthew. In between her shock at his arrival and her embarrassment at having her underwear strewn across the couch, the significance of his presence had begun to register. Perhaps there was a chance they could repair the damage caused by their quarrel. It occurred to Grace that she didn't want to lose Matthew's friendship. In two short months, he had become an integral part of her and Jason's life.

Matthew sat on the couch, stretching his arm along its back, and Grace joined him there a few feet away. His gaze moved appreciatively over her. Everything about her was soft and feminine, even her small, high-arched feet. He shifted. How on earth could looking at a woman's bare feet make his heart beat faster and his breath come quicker?

He frowned thoughtfully, then decided to get the trivial portion of the conversation over with. He reached for the folded paper in his shirt pocket.

"I have something for you, Grace."

Curious, she accepted the paper and unfolded it.

"It's the deed for Henshaw's lot. I bought it for you," he explained.

A quick scan of the document confirmed his words. She stared at him in astonishment. "For me?"

"For the school district," he amended, his fingers absently tapping the back of the sofa. "Even after the new school is finished and the old one torn down, the school should be able to use the extra space. There'll be room for a baseball diamond and soccer field. In the meantime, I want to contribute some more playground equipment to the school."

Grace meticulously refolded the deed. "That's very generous of you," she said quietly, meaning the compliment, but disappointed that a business matter had provoked Matthew's visit tonight.

"You're welcome." Perplexed, Matthew stared at Grace's subdued expression. He hadn't expected a brass band or a gushing burst of gratitude. But, dammit, was a smile too much to ask for?

Grimly he went to the next portion of the night's agenda. "My mother and father arrived back in town last night from their cruise. Dad's decided to keep Salvador Rodriguez on full-time."

"Oh, Matthew, that's wonderful." Again she spoke

sincerely, but disappointment made her voice thicken and her eyes grow moist.

Matthew continued. "Salvador's a good worker. Dad's glad to have him."

"The job means a lot to the Rodriguez family. I'm grateful you gave Salvador a chance."

I could do more, Grace. I want to do more. "I'm glad it worked out." The hand he rested on the back of the couch moved inexorably closer to her shoulder.

Grace was sure she could feel the heat emanating from Matthew's lean fingers as they rested innocently, scant inches from her. She chastised herself for her continuing physical awareness of Matthew Hollister. In that regard they had no common future. And the whole town of Banner's Point agreed with her.

"I'm sure you've noticed Brian and Jason are actually getting along."

"They *seem* to be getting along better," she agreed, frowning in concentration. "And it's nice to have the frog and worm plagues at an end. But I'm not so sure they've truly resolved their differences."

"You think this is just the lull before the storm?" A flicker of amusement danced in his dark eyes.

Grace didn't want to even hint at the closet episode, but knew there was no getting around it if she was to share some of the insights she'd gleaned from Jason about the debacle.

"I think they've decided to work together for a common goal." She found it easier to refer to the sensitive subject by addressing Matthew's right shoulder.

"You mean the night they decided to play match-maker?"

She nodded, never taking her eyes from his shoulder. It was so rugged looking. Under his tan shirt, it looked firm and powerful. It was the kind of shoulder a woman could lean on or, if circumstances warranted, cry on. It was also the kind of shoulder that hinted at strength and invited fantasies of hot, sultry nights and fevered touches.

"I had a talk with both Brian and Jason about that escapade." His eyes darkened at the sight of his hand all but touching her. It took little effort to imagine slipping the nightgown aside and caressing her soft, pale flesh.

"You talked to Jason about it? He didn't tell me." Briefly she felt a wave of distress that her son had confided in Matthew. She was Jason's mother. He should have confided in *her*.

Matthew read her feelings immediately. "I think our discussion fell under the 'man-to-man' category."

"Oh." She told herself it was unreasonable to feel jealous at being shut out from a man-to-man conversation. Especially when it was beginning to feel so right being with Matthew on a woman-to-man basis.

Matthew allowed himself the luxury of letting his fingertips trail across the beckoning pink satin. Intuitively he knew that beneath it lay skin just as soft, just as sensually stimulating.

"We needed to straighten out a couple of... points."

Quite suddenly his agenda for the night's discussion seemed to disintegrate. The sight of Grace sitting only inches from him with her bare knees demurely tucked together hammered at his self-control. Perspiration bathed his brow as he resisted the temptation to rip away the wisp of satin from her body.

The heat from Matthew's gaze joined with the fire of his touch and seeped through Grace's nightshirt, scorching her skin. "Wh-what points?"

He leaned toward her. "Points?" His voice was ragged and hungry.

"Yes..." Neither knew precisely what the yes was for. But each hoped.

His lips moved like a feverish whisper across her parted lips. "Oh, Lord, Grace. What you do to me...."

He kissed her. Slowly. With torturous control. And she yielded. Completely. With aching abandon.

Time continued. Elsewhere. In the fierce joining of their mouths, it held no power. The power came from the twin forces of their desperate yearning, their primal need to become one.

Matthew's hands moved eagerly across her. Satin and flesh. Sweetness and fulfillment. In her, he held it all. And he felt her hands upon him. Seeking. Needful. He moved his body over hers. His hands told him her satin nightshirt had ridden up to her waist, told him she was partially naked beneath him. His own body pounded with timeless hunger as he pressed against her.

Her mouth enslaved him. He wanted to kiss her everywhere. But he couldn't tear his lips from the hotly sweet cavern of her mouth. And so they kissed, feverishly, desperately. And in the insanity of the moment, Matthew managed to retain a thread of control. A man couldn't have a woman tremble beneath him as Grace trembled without knowing she was his for the taking.

But it had become more than lust or desire throbbing through Matthew's veins. Despite the insanity or perhaps because of it, he knew he wanted Grace in more ways then this. And just as surely as he knew that, he knew words not yet spoken needed to be said. He was determined that tonight there would be no misunderstandings between them. They needed the words.

Gently, lovingly he softened the pressure of his mouth. At his tender retreat, Grace's first reaction was to turn the aggressor. Her fingers tightened in his hair and she pulled him to her. Matthew's mouth broke contact with hers and he rained quick kisses on her flushed forehead and cheeks.

"Darling, we've got to talk."

Chapter Nine

Husky and raw, his voice barely penetrated Grace's dazed mind. Her eyelids drifted open. Matthew's eyes, burning with barely banked male need, pinned her. Instinctively she tried to pull away but his embrace tightened.

The full implication of their intimate position came crashing down on her. Dear God in heaven, she was sprawled shamelessly beneath him. Her skin flamed. With horror she realized her nightshirt had become unbuttoned and she was virtually naked. She pressed her eyelids tightly shut. This was a nightmare. This hadn't really happened. Not again. Why, this was a repeat of their disastrous encounter in the closet. No, this was worse. At least then she'd managed to keep her clothes on.

"Don't."

At his whispered command, Grace's eyes again

opened. Her mouth moved, but no words came. She wanted to tell him to get off her. She wanted to tell him to get out and never come back. She wanted to tell him...not to stop what he'd begun.

"Don't what?"

"Don't shut me out, darling."

Then he startled her by abruptly shifting their positions. In one swift movement, she ended up on his lap. Her hands flew to the front of her gaping nightshirt, but his hands raced hers there and began to smoothly button it.

"The first time we met you were wearing pearl buttons." Emotion thickened his voice.

Grace barely had time to assimilate his words before he stunned her with a hard, swift kiss and a fierce hug.

"Now we talk."

Talk? Who had any strength left to talk? Her lips tingled with the throbbing imprint of his mouth. Her breasts ached and her lower body hummed with expectations that were clearly going to go unmet. And Matthew Hollister wanted to *talk*.

"Grace, I don't think either of us said what we really meant the night of the carnival. I know I didn't, and I hope maybe you didn't, either."

She licked her lips. "I—I meant what I said, but somehow it didn't come out right."

"After I cooled down, I began thinking about what you'd told me." His arms tightened around her. "First I want to apologize for losing my temper. I don't usually. But it's kind of hard on a man's ego to hear that the woman in his arms isn't seriously interested in him.''

''I meant that the other way around,'' she confessed.

''That I couldn't be serious about you?''

''You yourself said what we were doing was a mistake. And...and I know you're right. I know there can never be anything lasting between us. But I need the 'lasting,' Matthew. I just can't give myself lightly. Only I don't know how to kill this...this passion we seem to spark in each other.''

The severe lines marking his features softened. ''Don't you know you can't fight nature?''

She didn't smile. ''Is that what's drawing us together, Matthew? Just nature?''

''Perhaps in the beginning. But I think if you gave us a chance, we could share something more than hormones.''

''And everything standing between us? Do we just pretend it doesn't exist?''

''What's standing between us, Grace? Our sons?''

''They're a part of the problem,'' she agreed.

''Maybe not. Jason and Brian have spent a lot of time together without any flare-ups. I do admit some of the reason they're getting along is because Brian has decided you'd make a terrific mother and Jason seems intrigued with the notion of having me for a father.''

''You discussed becoming Jason's father with him?''

''Indirectly.''

As if by unspoken agreement, Matthew and Grace eased apart on the couch. He missed their closeness, but decided he wanted to look into the turbulent gray eyes of the woman who was fast becoming the most important person in his life.

"Indirectly? Either you did or you didn't," she challenged, eyes flashing, not at all happy with Matthew for discussing something so personal with her son.

"Then we did," he acknowledged quietly. "Look, Grace, Jason is ten years old. He's at the stage where he's looking for a little male guidance. It's not a reflection on your mothering ability. It's just a fact of life."

"And of course you know all about the facts of life?" Grace hated her shrewishness, but she couldn't seem to help herself. She couldn't—*wouldn't*—let her son's need for a masculine influence be the determining factor in her romantic relationships.

Matthew's gaze narrowed. "I know enough about the facts of life to know that any time now you and I are going to make love. And it'd be a damned shame for us to be strangers when we do."

The color fled from Grace's face. "You presume too much."

"I *presume* right, Grace. Look at yourself and look at me. Right now we're seconds away from doing something irrevocable, something that could reshape both our lives."

Her gaze dropped and she sucked in her breath. Her legs were completely exposed. Her nightshirt had been incorrectly fastened and beneath its thin surface the telltale evidence of her aroused state was clearly outlined.

Unwillingly, her gaze went to Matthew. His dark hair had been mussed and the evidence of his desire was also obvious beneath his disheveled clothing. He was right. It wouldn't take much to ignite the powder keg of their seething emotions. And they would be strangers.

Her solemn gaze returned to his flushed face. "I meant it when I said desire wasn't enough."

"And because I'm a man, you think it's enough for me?"

She shook her head. "I don't know what's enough for either of us."

Unshed tears gave Grace's eyes a luminescent sheen. Matthew reached out and soothed away one drop with his fingertip. He could feel her drawing away from him, boarding up her emotions. And because he knew he would be gone in the morning, he decided to ease up. Even though his instincts called for it, this was not the time to storm the lady's battlements. It was too soon.

It had been only since the night of the Halloween carnival, the night of their brief madness in a darkened closet, that he had come to realize what Grace Banner could mean to him. What they could mean to each other. He studied her pale features and understood this was not the moment to make demands. He had his own reservations about the two of them becoming intimately involved. Neither of them could take and give lightly—emotionally or physically. But there was something about this quietly dignified, shy and yet surprisingly spirited woman that would not let him go.

He forced his tense muscles to relax. He'd begun D.D. from a back corner of a defunct wrecking yard. Persistence, determination and knowing when to back away had paid off. Though hardly romantic, he had the feeling those same precepts would work for him now.

"How about being my friend, Grace? Can we start there?"

"Your friend?"

He could see he'd surprised her. "Yeah, why don't we ask of ourselves what we've demanded from our sons?"

Grace's delicate brows drew together thoughtfully as she considered his request. "Despite all the other…" She gestured with a small hand.

And Matthew interpreted "the other" to mean the rock-hard hunger he felt for her. He couldn't help smiling. The lady had a knack for understatement.

"I would like to be your friend," she finished, her voice scarcely above a whisper.

"Good. I need a favor." He tamped down a grin when her eyes widened at his blunt request.

"Okay. What can I do for you?"

Oh, lady, you can take my hand and lead me into tomorrow. A lot of tomorrows.

"I'm going to be out of town for a few days on business. There's some snags I have to work through on moving my corporate headquarters. Mom and Dad have offered to keep Brian. But as hard as it is to believe, he's asked if he can stay with you and Jason.''

''You're right. It is hard to believe. What do you think they're up to?''

''Knowing my son and yours, it could be anything.''

''More matchmaking?'' Grace asked uneasily.

''Could be, but as long as we're on to them, what can they do? Besides I still think them spending time together is the best way to end their feud.''

''Matthew, has Jason ever talked to you about his father? I mean, in the beginning Jason really resented your moving to the Point and now he seems to have changed his feelings about your being here. What caused the shift?''

Matthew heard the unasked question. Why didn't Jason feel disloyal in switching his boyish affections to a man many people regarded as his father's enemy? And that was the one subject Matthew refused to get into tonight with Grace. Not when he sensed her resistance toward his wavering. Another time they'd lay the ghost of Blake Banner to rest.

''I think Jason is coming to terms with his feelings about me. It's surprising how much the scouting has helped. He's been able to see me in a relaxed setting, heard me tell some corny jokes and burn several dozen lumpy pancakes. I'm no longer an unknown entity. I'm just another father.''

"I see." She wondered if life could really be that simple. It didn't seem possible. "Matthew?"

"Yes, Grace?"

"Why...why did you run for Congress against Blake? You'd never been involved in politics before."

Matthew's features changed dramatically. His dark brows contracted and his eyes narrowed. "That election happened in another lifetime; I don't see any point in rehashing it now."

Was Matthew ashamed of his reasons for seeking public office? She had to know once and for all how deep his rivalry with her late husband was. She took a deep breath. "Was it because of Blake? Did you need to try and beat him one last time?" *Please let it have been the last time.*

Matthew could feel a low, simmering anger building within him. He wasn't used to having to explain himself to anyone. Not since Cathy's death had he been forced to open himself up to the kind of emotional intimacy Grace was demanding. Why was she pushing so hard now for answers that he knew would alienate her from him?

"Before that damned election, before Cathy...died, we lived in Boise. I commuted by company jet to L.A. where D.D.'s headquarters is located. The political party I'm affiliated with had another candidate slated to run against Blake. Unfortunately that candidate was caught in a very embarrassing episode with a woman other than his wife.

"I was second choice, a dark horse to run against

Blake." He paused and studied his hands. "Yes, the fact that I would be running against Blake Banner was an irresistible lure. But—" he brought his head up and held Grace with his gaze "—before the campaign was over, it ceased to matter *who* my opponent was. I began to care about the issues. That's it. Case closed."

She wanted to believe him, but she couldn't—not completely.

"I'll have my housekeeper bring Brian's things over tomorrow."

"All right." Grace found herself feeling a little lost. The abrupt change from passionate lovers to sparring partners then pals was difficult to adjust to.

She found herself leaning forward. Despite her doubts and fears, or perhaps because of them, she needed to feel close to him, needed to touch him. She was grateful when he met her halfway.

What harm could there be in a parting kiss? His mouth covered hers with careful intent. She discovered the passion had lingered close to the surface, ready to spill over with the sensual caress of tongue against tongue. But she'd lost control once tonight and didn't dare tempt fate with so bold a move. Matthew must have shared her hesitation for his lips moved across her with the lightest pressure.

Several moments passed. When they drew apart, their softened gazes embraced long after the kiss itself had ended. Together they stood, her hand locked securely in his, and they moved into the living room.

Matthew accepted his coat and put it on in silence. They paused side by side, facing the closed door.

Walking through that door and leaving Grace tonight was the last thing on the planet Matthew wanted to do. He dared not let his thoughts drift to what it was he *did* want to do. His hand went to the doorknob, which turned with well-oiled smoothness. Calling on every scrap of strength he could summon, he stepped into the night.

The porch light trapped millions of swirling snowflakes in a yellowish prism of light. And standing in her doorway, Grace Banner forgot. Forgot there was a town full of people who believed that she and this man didn't belong together. Forgot that her loyalty to a man no longer alive forbade involvement with this one.

"Matthew."

At the sound of her voice, he turned and somehow found her in his arms. This kiss was raw, desperate wild. As wild as the icy flurries of snow whipping about them.

"Oh, Lord, honey. You're barefoot and practically naked. Get inside before you freeze to death."

How could she freeze? She was on fire, and his raspy words, hot and steamy against her throat, only fueled that fire. "In a minute." Her arms clung to him.

"Now, sweetheart. Now." His hands quickly separated them, and with an economy of movement, he deposited her inside her living room. Then he closed the heavy front door between them.

Matthew sucked in a great gulp of cold air and leaned his perspiring forehead against the door. On the other side of the closed door, Grace pantomimed his frustrated gesture. A full minute passed before Matthew straightened, left the meager protection of the front porch and strode into the night.

Dazedly Grace returned to the family room. She looked at the coffee table covered with her silky lingerie and wondered blankly how it had gotten there.

Chapter Ten

"Teeth all brushed?" Grace smiled at the faint mint smudges around Jason and Brian's freshly washed faces.

Brian grinned. "Yeah, no cavity bug could live after what we just put them through."

Grace's eyes sparkled with affection. Brian's broad grin was a miniature of his father's. Her gaze drifted to Jason. Both boys were dressed for bed in red and blue thermal-woven pajamas. They looked adorable. Too bad Matthew had missed Thanksgiving with them.

It had been a most unusual day, including as it had both Jason's and Brian's grandparents. The Banners and Hollisters—together for Thanksgiving Dinner. No doubt about it, they were living in an age of miracles.

"Well, now that you've had your showers and brushed your teeth, it's off to bed with you."

"Can Brian and I play one more game of Battleship? There's no school tomorrow."

Grace followed the boys into Jason's bedroom. The hammock Matthew had installed looked as if it belonged in her son's room. Jason and Brian had taken turns sleeping in it.

"Play a couple of games."

"All right!" they chorused enthusiastically.

Grace gave Jason a quick hug and tousled his honey-colored hair. "Night, honey." He was young enough to return the hug and old enough to be self-conscious about it.

"Night, Brian." She gave the dark-eyed boy an affectionate hug and then couldn't resist ruffling his hair, too. His arms went around her waist for a vigorous if brief squeeze.

"Good night, Mrs. Banner."

"Mrs. Banner" sounded so formal. Yet she could hardly invite him to call her Grace. The boys began setting up their game, and she slipped from the room.

Almost an hour later she was settled in her own bed, quietly turning the pages of Blake's high school yearbook. So much innocence, so much enthusiasm. The black-and-white annual bore mute testimony to a simpler, slower-paced period of time.

She turned a thick, glossy page and looked into the impossibly young face of Matthew Hollister, a Matthew without faint lines creasing his dark eyes. He looked eager. Fresh faced, square jawed—the kind of young man she would expect to see throwing a football on a crisp fall afternoon or flirting madly with a lithe, long-haired teenage girl or helping a little old lady across a busy intersection. You'd trust a boy like that with your daughter and your mother and your dog.

Decent. That was the word.

Two pages later Grace stared into her late husband's blond handsome features. She ran her finger tip lightly across the smooth, boyish planes of his face. Blake. Gone. Forever. A light extinguished. Had they been happy those last few hectic years? She couldn't remember their sharing time alone together. Political ambition had seduced Blake more thoroughly than another woman could have.

She turned the page. There was Blake again, in a tuxedo at some kind of formal dance. In his arms was a lovely young woman in a strapless ball gown. Grace smiled. Odd how the girls always looked years older than the boys. Midway through the large annual, she continued to slowly turn the pages.

She stopped when she came to a picture of Matthew at another formal school dance. His companion was a girl who looked uncannily similar to the one Blake had been with. Intrigued, Grace flicked back to the earlier photograph. It was the same girl.

Her curiosity aroused, she turned to the section of the yearbook containing individual class pictures. Most of the small portraits were exuberantly autographed. She located the mystery girl in the P's. Linda

Pond. The message beneath it read—"So glad M.H. didn't come between us. Love, Linda."

Grace read the not-so-cryptic words three times before closing the yearbook.

When the phone at her bedside rang, a feeling of inevitability swept over Grace.

"Hi." The simple greeting pulsed with rich vitality. "I miss you."

For a moment the healing magic of his voice lightened Grace's pensive mood. "I've missed you, too."

"I'll be home tomorrow. I'm sorry I missed Thanksgiving."

Grace stared unseeingly at the ceiling. "Have you talked to your parents today?"

"Yeah, and I caught holy heck for letting business take priority over Brian *and* you and Jason. I could hardly believe it when Dad said the Banners and Hollisters had shared Thanksgiving supper. What's going on?"

"I'll let you figure it out when you get home," she replied, not wanting to get into the subject of how both sets of grandparents seemed to be doing a little matchmaking of their own.

"That'll be tomorrow night around seven. Will you pick me up at the airport?"

Grace hesitated. Perhaps it was best she slowed down her deepening involvement with Matthew. Twice she'd almost made love to him. He was still a stranger to her. She really didn't know what demons drove him. And she didn't seem to have the courage to find out.

"I'll bring the boys; they'd be disappointed if they missed a trip to the airport."

Eight hundred miles away in his Los Angeles suite, Matthew heard the wariness in Grace's soft voice. In the two weeks they'd been apart, he'd lost ground with her. He could feel her restraint toward him over the phone.

For Matthew the past fourteen days spent hassling contractors, attorneys and his board of directors had reenforced the wisdom of moving his business headquarters to Idaho Falls. The thirteen nights had reenforced his strong feelings for Grace. With a jolt, he realized he was counting on a commitment from her for the future. Their future. He had no intention of letting her drift away from him.

Along with the emotional pull he felt toward her, he was also feeling some powerful urges of a more physical nature. Just hearing her voice long distance made his body hurt with hunger. When the distance between them was no longer hundreds of miles but meager inches, it was going to take every scrap of control he could muster not to—

"Matthew, are you still there?"

"Oh, yeah."

"You sound tired. You'd better get to sleep."

Matthew glared into the receiver. Tired, hell. His body felt as if it had enough untapped energy to scale a mountain. "I'm okay. Say, if you wanted to come alone to the airport, we could go out to dinner and—"

"The boys would love to go out to eat. How does pizza sound?"

"Swell, Grace. It sounds just swell."

"See you tomorrow, then. Good night."

Matthew heard a click, and he hung up the phone somberly. Tomorrow it would be. He scowled. Tomorrow Ms. Grace Banner would discover any and all barriers she'd erected between them were going to come tumbling down. Then his scowl faded. Banner's Point was hardly Jericho. And he was no Joshua. That was fine. He had no intention of letting seven days go by before he'd stormed Grace's defenses. It was time the lady learned she didn't need them, with him.

Grace couldn't ignore the surge of heat that swept through her when Matthew walked across the small Idaho Falls airport to her and the boys.

His tall, lean body radiated tautly leashed energy. Dressed in a charcoal-gray expertly tailored suit and carrying a dark briefcase and heavy gray wool coat, he resembled a modern-day gladiator. But it was his implacable, almost ruthless facial expression and not his clothes that made Grace think of arenas, Christians—and lions.

"Boy, Dad looks mad," breathed Brian. Grace silently concurred.

When Matthew reached them, he dropped his coat and briefcase on the airport's carpeted floor. Instantly he had Brian in his arms. The hug he gave his son was bone crushing and was returned wholeheartedly. He released Brian and then startled Jason with an only marginally milder version of Brian's hug.

A lump rose in Grace's throat. She tried to resist her feelings at seeing her son embraced in Matthew's unabashed warmth, but she was unsuccessful. For in a frozen corner that she hadn't even known existed in her heart, she felt a life-giving thawing, an elemental awakening. Moments before she'd been aware of Jason's unspoken sense of loss when Brian had been swept into his father's arms. In less than a minute Matthew had banished that loss.

Matthew gave Jason one final squeeze before releasing him and standing up. Something about the determined gleam in the man's eyes made Grace back away. Then there was no time left for retreat. Matthew's firm mouth came down hard on hers and his powerful arms gathered her to his broad chest. Faintly she thought she heard Jason's and Brian's boyish cheers before a dull roar much like the sound of a jet taking off filled her ears.

She was in the eye of a sensual hurricane and it was heaven. Her reservations about Matthew Hollister certainly weren't physical in nature. No. She had no reservations of that kind about the man presently kissing the stuffing from her boneless body.

She felt the pressure of his mouth lighten and became aware of the novel sensation of tingling patches of skin, patches where his lips had strung brief kisses over her face and throat. She was thankful that he still held her. It would have been embarrassing to have collapsed on the airport floor because her knees had failed her.

"Like I said on the phone, I've missed you. A lot." His words fell like hot honey against her throat.

"Ah…ah, yes…"

He squeezed her tightly, his dark eyes boring into hers. "Tell me."

"What?" she asked in bewilderment.

"How much you've missed me."

Grace was stunned to see uncertainty in his intense gaze. And even though she was thinking very seriously of easing herself from Matthew's life, she couldn't bear to see the proud man vulnerable.

Still a captive of his embrace, she smiled softly. "I've missed you a lot, you crazy man. Now let me go before we scandalize our sons."

His head bent forward and he gave her another kiss—a kiss so tender, so innately loving that it brought tears to her eyes. And when the kiss—part heaven, yet grounded by the earthly flesh that bound them—was over, he didn't let her go. Instead he called over his shoulder for the two boys to pick up his coat and briefcase.

With his arm around her, they retrieved his luggage and walked to her car. He had to release her for a moment when he noticed Idaho Falls was covered in snow and he needed to put his coat on. Once at the car, the boys piled into the back seat.

Grace reached into her coat pocket and fished

around for her keys. "Would you mind driving, Matthew? I go pretty slow on slick roads."

Their eyes met, then his gaze dropped to encompass the rest of her. She had the distinct feeling he was seeing her without her clothes on. She trembled. Didn't the man have any consideration? It was freezing outside. How dared he undress her with his eyes? She'd catch pneumonia.

"Slow is the only way to drive on black ice. But I don't mind driving if the roads bother you."

You bother me! What am I going to do about that, Matthew Hollister? "Thank you."

"My pleasure, Grace."

The pizza parlor was crowded with other families celebrating the Thanksgiving break. The video arcade games, the college football game on television and laughing conversations around them should have broken the sensual spell in which Matthew seemed determined to bind her. But Grace doubted an avalanche could have pried his hypnotic gaze from her.

And it didn't matter at all that she had decided to be immune to his appeal. Throughout dinner his conversation had been remarkably commonplace, in no way referring to the feminine hunger he aroused in her. They sat alone at the table over the remains of a deep-dish pizza while the boys tried their luck with arcade games. And Grace wondered if perhaps *she* was the one sending out the X-rated thoughts.

Why did Matthew have to be so rugged, so handsome? A tiny furrow marred her brow when she re-

alized there had been a time when she hadn't thought
of him as handsome. She must have been suffering
from distorted vision because it was very clear to her
that, had he ever gone to Hollywood, the man seated
across from her could have had a career as a cine-
matic heartthrob.

"What's the frown for?"

Grace blushed. "Just thinking."

"About what?"

"Oh, I don't know—life, I guess."

"And thinking about life makes you frown?" His
dark eyes were warm with gentle amusement.
"You've got to lighten up, honey. Christmas is coming, the season of good cheer and mistletoe."

Grace laughed. "The season of overspending and
overeating. Of huge Christmas card lists and—"

"Stop—where's your holiday spirit?"

"It's too soon to be thinking about Christmas."

"No way. I'm looking forward to an old-fashioned
Christmas with all the trimmings."

"You sound like our boys."

"I like the sound of that." His strong hands
reached out across the small table and captured hers.

"What?" It was hard to think coherently with tiny
explosions of heat ricocheting through her body.

"'Our boys.'"

Again his dark gaze bound her to him. "Uh,
well…" The tip of her tongue worried her bottom lip.

"Grace, I have an idea."

Oh, I bet you do, Mr. Bedroom Eyes! "What's that?"

"Let's take my dad's horse-drawn sleigh up to the hills and cut a couple of fresh trees."

Grace met his dark eyes and forced herself to remember her reasons for putting distance between herself and this man. A man who might be using her in some misguided way to gain a final victory over Blake. There would be no shared cutting of Christmas trees for them. No more outings to pizza parlors. No nothing.

"I don't think—"

He interrupted her. "The boys would love it," he pressed, shamelessly playing on her love for them. "I've already mentioned it, and I'd hate to disappoint them."

"I don't want to disappoint them, either, but—"

"Brian and I will drop by after breakfast."

A feeling of emptiness cut through Grace when she realized Brian would of course be going home tonight with his father. She blinked back tears, stunned at how much she'd already come to love the boy who'd become a vital part of her and Jason's life. The house would seem so empty without the two children exchanging their irrepressible brand of boyish camaraderie.

Jason and Brian returned to the table, insisting their parents play a couple of arcade games with them. Grace pushed back her chair and followed the three laughing males. She had the feeling her neatly laid-out future was in serious jeopardy.

As she handed Jason several quarters, she looked into his excited green eyes. And she wondered if it really mattered that Matthew might be using her for his own ends. She'd never seen her son so happy. It was a daunting discovery to realize her decision to expunge Matthew from her life would have a major effect on Jason. Her son was squarely in the middle of her future with or without Matthew Hollister.

Of course she wasn't certain Matthew had anything permanent between them on his mind. How lasting was his need to have what had been Blake's?

Her eyes went to Brian. She loved him. It shook her to understand she couldn't have loved him more if he were her own biological child. Did it matter so much that Matthew's feelings for her might be sparked by a long-term grudge against her former husband?

Her confused gaze went to Matthew as he concentrated enthusiastically on the animated screen of tricky blue mazes. Unable to stop herself, she stepped closer to him, reaching out to touch his arm. In him might lie heartbreak and disillusionment, but she seemed unable to resist the good he might hold for her.

He looked up from the screen with laughing eyes, and she felt her heart expand with emotion. As long as she lived, she would always remember this moment, the way Matthew looked tonight. Boyishly alive, ruggedly handsome and available—on his terms. Could she live with those terms?

"Come on, honey. Give it a try. We can't let these pip-squeaks think we old folks can't keep up with them."

A strong arm pulled her into the magic circle of Matthew's embrace and he gave her a quick hug before turning her to face the screen again.

"Put in another quarter, Jason. Your mother's going to teach us men how the game is played." His lips brushed her forehead in a gentle kiss, and her ears alone caught his next huskily murmured statement. "You don't have to prove anything to me, darling. I know you're hot stuff. And soon, very soon, we're going to set the whole damned world on fire."

Grace, Matthew, Jason and Brian encircled the perfectly shaped pine. It stood alone on a snow-covered knoll, its long-needled limbs weighted with iridescent mounds of sparkling snowflakes.

"We won't find another one prettier than this," said Matthew, his deep voice filling the forest's awesome stillness.

"No, we won't," agreed Grace, stamping her booted feet in the deep snow to keep the circulation flowing. Puffs of condensed air punctuated her words.

"Get the chain saw, Brian."

"Wait." Grace put her mittened hand on Matthew's coat sleeve.

He turned to her. "Wait for what?"

"Let's not cut down the tree, Matthew," she

pleaded in a rush, embarrassed by her sentimentality, but unable to help herself. "It's so beautiful growing naturally. I don't want to kill it."

"Oh, brother," muttered Jason.

Matthew stared down at her with consternation. "Grace, we've just spent the past three hours looking at some four hundred trees and rejecting them because they didn't measure up to your standards. They were to big. They were too small. They leaned to the left or to the right. They were too thin on the top or the bottom, or—"

"I was there, Matthew," she interjected dryly. "I remember."

"Now we find the perfect tree. There's not one damned thing wrong with it and you—you don't want me to *kill* it?" Amused exasperation laced his words.

"It seems a shame to punish the tree because it's so beautiful."

Matthew stared at her incredulously and then threw back his head and laughed. The boys joined him, hooting and chasing each other in the snow.

Then Matthew grabbed Grace and kissed her soundly. His lusty kiss ended with a loud smack. "You heard your mother, boys. Pack up the chain saw. The good fairy of Peninsula Elementary has decreed this tree will see more than one Christmas."

As they waded through the deep snow arm-in-arm, Grace turned to Matthew. "You're not upset?"

"No way. The fun was in all of us being together

and having a good time." He chuckled softly. "We must have thrown a million snowballs."

"At least," Grace replied, recalling the avalanche of ricocheting missiles that had flown between the four of them.

"Jason, why don't you break out the thermos? I'd like another cup of your mom's hot spiced cider, wouldn't you?"

"You bet! And some of those doughnuts she made, too."

"Yeah, don't forget the doughnuts," chimed in Brian.

Soon they were feasting on the cinnamon-glazed pastries and gulping down the hot cider. Swallowing the last of his drink, Matthew closed his eyes in appreciation. "Lord, Grace. You sure know how to cook."

"Thank you."

He reached for another doughnut. "It surprises me."

"That I can cook?"

He shook his head. "No, that you can find the time to cook." He smiled crookedly. "It takes me almost an hour to make cocoa."

She couldn't help laughing softly at his rueful expression. "When Jason was younger, he used to have all kinds of allergies. I found that when I made things from scratch he got along better than on packaged foods. After a while, I started to enjoy cooking just for the fun of it. It was relaxing. Silly, huh?"

"No, not silly." Matthew gazed deeply into Grace's dove-gray eyes. "It's just one more facet of your uniqueness."

"My uniqueness?"

"Yeah. Like the way you blink sometimes when I say something that throws you. Or your dedication to your job. Or the capacity you seemingly have to love both our sons equally."

Grace swallowed. "Please don't..."

"Don't what?"

Don't make me admit that I've fallen in love with you. Deeply shaken, Grace turned from his stare.

During today's outing, she had deliberately blanked out her doubts about Matthew's motives, choosing instead to enjoy the moment—lightly. But Matthew's seriousness, his habit of leading their conversations onto more intimate tracks than she could endure made it impossible for her to deny her love for him. And she found it just as impossible to keep her doubts about him at bay.

She jammed her hands into her coat pockets. "Don't flatter me; I embarrass easily."

Matthew swore under his breath. She was doing it again. Destroying their close moments with invisible but nevertheless solid barriers. He glanced at their sons, frolicking in the deep snow. Now was hardly the moment to tell Grace of his love. He frowned. He did love her, dammit. And he wanted to tell her that he had found the courage to love again. And to help her understand that within her existed the same courage.

"Then maybe it's time you learned to accept a compliment, honey." He put his arm around her shoulders and again looked over at Jason and Brian. "Come on, boys. Let's get this show on the road. We've got to get back to town so we can buy a couple of Christmas trees."

They began organizing the sleigh for the return ride home. "I drove past one lot that sells potted trees. I've got a hunch that's the kind we're going to end up with this year."

Grace tried to ignore the physical sensations Matthew's closeness awakened and to concentrate instead on the instructions he was giving the boys.

"Sit up on the driver's platform and you can take turns handling the reins."

"All right!" they chimed in unison, scaling the high driver's seat.

Grace stared up at the two beaming boys uneasily. "Ah, Matthew, I don't want to be a spoilsport, but do you think Brian and Jason are old enough and experienced enough to manage?" The two sleigh horses looked about ten feet tall and had hooves the size of manhole covers.

"Sure. Dad filled in for me as scout master with the Webelos while I was gone. I know they've had at least five meetings showing the boys how to handle old Meg and Daisy. They'll do just fine."

Before she had time to realize what was happening,

Grace found herself tucked neatly beneath a thick plaid blanket with Matthew Hollister as her sole companion.

"Cosy, huh?"

"Very." Cozy as in a raging inferno, thought Grace, knowing she was unable to cope with Matthew's nearness.

"You're too far away."

"I'm practically on your lap!"

"Yeah. It's the 'practically' that's the problem, honey. Come here."

"Oh!"

"Oh, yeah," he growled against her ear.

"B-but, the boys will—"

"Learn that giving and receiving affection is a natural, good thing. I want them to know that being a man doesn't mean keeping feelings inside. It's taken me a lifetime to realize that. I want to save them some time."

"But, Matthew, I—"

"Shh, just let me hold you." And he did. All the way home.

Later in the evening they found the lot selling live trees, and they bought two. That night they decorated Grace's Christmas tree, and the following night they decorated Matthew's.

For Grace the next few days passed in bittersweet tranquillity. Matthew took several days off work to spend time with her and the boys. They shopped, strung miles of outdoor lights on both houses and

built "awesome" snowmen. Matthew and the boys
made a series of interconnecting snow caves. And all
of them kept and told endless secrets.

To those looking in from the outside, it seemed as
if the Banners and the Hollisters were living in idyllic
harmony. But inside, Grace was living on the cutting
edge of her emotions. She could feel Matthew stalking her, closing the distance between them. He
wanted her. She would have to have been a lifeless
statue not to realize that. And Lord help her, she
wanted him just as desperately. Physically.

Could that be enough for her?

Chapter Eleven

"Mom!"

Grace looked up from the Christmas card list she was updating. "I'm in the kitchen."

Jason came barrelling into the room. "Brian phoned. His dad's going to be here any minute to pick me up."

"Do you have all your gear packed?"

"Yeah, it's gonna be great tonight. I've never slept in a snow cave before."

Grace eyed her excited son with a smile. He probably wouldn't appreciate hearing it, but he looked very cute in his dark blue uniform. "Few of us have. Did you pack your thermal underwear?"

"Ah, Mom, that's personal."

"So's frostbite. Did you bring the heavy sleeping bag up from the basement?"

"Yeah. Hey, Mr. Hollister just drove up. I gotta go, Mom."

By the time Grace pushed back her chair from the table, Jason was already out the door. She'd never seen him so excited. She watched through the kitchen window as Matthew helped her son load his camping gear inside the trunk of his perfectly restored 1967 black Camaro. Then both of them returned to the house.

"What did you forget?" Grace asked, unable to keep from staring at Matthew.

She discovered there was truth to the old saying about men in uniform. On Matthew even a khaki scout uniform looked terribly sexy. There was something about seeing a muscular physique in—

"My toothbrush, a flashlight, towel, some old newspapers, a plastic trash bag and—"

Grace held up a hand to halt his apparently unending flow of forgotten items. "Do you have a list?"

"Right here."

"Then go to it, sport."

Jason dashed out of the kitchen at a dead run. Grace turned to Matthew. "Do they really need all that just to sleep out in your backyard?"

"It's in the manual," he returned, a slow smile working its way across his mouth. "You do remember that I'm a man who believes in going by the book."

All at once Grace was reminded of the October

morning they had fished from Matthew's dock and
the dog-eared booklet he'd followed.

Grace's wave of nostalgia dissolved when she realized she was retreating with each step Matthew took
toward her. This was her kitchen and no one was
going to intimidate—

"Where're you running to, honey?" His voice was
a velvet rasp.

"No—" She cleared her throat. "Nowhere."

"Good." He closed the distance between them and
his hands cupped her shoulders.

"Matthew, I don't know what you have in mind,
but Jason could come downstairs any minute and—"

Matthew's smile reeked of masculine satisfaction.
"I don't think so."

Grace's eyes narrowed. "Why not?"

"I added a few items to his list. I don't think he'll
be coming out of his bedroom for a good long time.
Now come here."

He pulled her forcibly into his arms, and Grace
found herself the recipient of a kiss that was both
sweet and faintly savage. And though her mind cried
for restraint, her arms crept around his neck. She
could feel herself melting against him—from within,
where tiny frissons of desire fevered the blood dash-
ing through her veins and from without, where the
solid reality of his hard body imprinted itself against
hers.

The heat, the fire was everywhere. Everywhere she
had been designed to feel. Demanding, relentless—

chaining. Matthew Hollister had become the embodiment of dark desire and a part of her existed only to satisfy that desire.

"That's it, darling. Let go." His hot, moist breath moved along her throat.

"Oh, Matthew," sighed Grace, feeling herself surrender utterly to his potent power over her. "I want to, but—"

"Shh, I know. We need to be alone, honey. Really alone. We need to say all the words. It's just that times like now, I forget you haven't quite caught up with me."

His hands smoothed her blouse and then dropped to her waist where he held her in a light embrace.

"Caught up with you?"

"Yeah." His roughened fingertip stroked her cheek. "With how I feel about you, Grace. Sometimes I feel as if I've made a quantum jump into the future, but you're still standing in the past."

"I don't know what you mean."

His gaze filled with tenderness and he gathered her hands in his. Gently he massaged the rings Blake had given her. "Jump, darling."

"What?"

"Jump with me. Into the future. I've found out how to do it. You close your eyes and let go. Everything else takes care of itself. Our love for each other can solve any problem."

She stared at the forceful man towering above her,

and the part of her that feared him and his motives found other meaning for his words.

"Let go" of her pride? "Close her eyes" to how Matthew might still be trying to compete with Blake? "Jump" into an uncertain future where she wasn't loved for herself?

"You mean let go of Blake's memory?" she asked in a hollow voice.

Grace's question jarred Matthew. He'd forgotten that she'd ever belonged to another man. Somehow his growing love for her had made her new to him. And he had felt that same newness in himself. As if there'd been no other woman in his life before Grace, and there would be no other woman after her.

"You'll have to let go of his memory at some point, if you want to get on with the business of living."

Grace took a deep breath. Maybe it was time to let Matthew know she wasn't the kind of woman to let herself be used by any man for any reason. "How do I let go, Matthew?"

"For a start you can take off Blake's wedding rings. He's gone."

Is he? Is he really? she wanted to ask. Instead she raised her chin. "All right." The rings came off slowly, stubbornly. She laid them on the kitchen counter. The fancy settings looked strangely out of place against the clean blue tiles.

"Next?" Her voice was flat, without emotion.

Matthew stared intently at Grace, utterly baffled by

her strangely subdued behavior. What was wrong with her? Why did she look as if someone had just shot her pet puppy?

"Grace, honey, what's—"

"Come on, Matthew, what's next? Isn't this where you ask me to marry you? Or is having a brief affair with Blake Banner's widow enough for you?"

"An affair? Have you lost your mind?"

She continued ruthlessly. "Do you want me to declare my everlasting love? Or is it enough that I tell you I love you more than I ever loved Blake? How much do you need, Matthew? How much before you can celebrate your final triumph over Blake?"

Matthew staggered back, his face twisted with pain. It took him a moment to catch his breath. For one split second he stared at Grace's frozen features and wondered. Just how pure had been his attraction to Blake's widow? In the next instant he knew he didn't deserve her doubts.

"Yeah, that's what I want to hear all right. Tell me. Tell me how much you love me, Grace."

"I do, you know. That's what makes this so unbearable." Tears streamed unheeded down her cheeks.

"*Love me?*" He forced himself to laugh. It was a forlorn sound. "You don't know the meaning of the word. *I* loved, Grace. You. I *loved* you, dammit. And all the time you thought I was only out to somehow use you to beat Blake?" He shook his head in weary defeat.

"You want to know what makes this all so damned funny, Grace? When we first met, I thought I was the one who was emotionally crippled, who wasn't ready to love again. You were the one who seemed whole. And I was haunted by the possibility I wasn't." He broke off and rubbed a hand across his eyes.

"I didn't think I was worthy of you, Grace. Isn't that a joke? I didn't think I was man enough to offer you what you needed. And it turns out that you aren't woman enough for me. You're so damned riddled with insecurity that you can't see what it's all about when a man loves a woman." His eyes darkened. "And a woman loves a man."

For a long moment he stared at her. Then he looked away, as if the sight of her hurt his eyes. He reached for the rings on the countertop. "You'd better hang on to these, Grace. You're not ready to let go of them, or the past."

He pressed Blake's rings into her soft flesh, closing her fingers firmly over the sharp stones. His dark eyes glittered with savage intensity. "They won't keep you warm at night, Grace."

She read the pain and disillusionment in his dark eyes and knew. Knew how terribly she'd wronged him. "Matthew, please. Maybe I misunderstood. Let's talk about—"

"I got it all! Man, that was the longest list I ever saw. Why do I need a compass to sleep in your backyard, anyway, Mr. Hollister?" Jason's arrival silenced Grace's pleas before she could voice them.

"So you don't get lost, son. Come on, we'd better get going. The guys are waiting for us." The door opened and closed behind them with quiet finality.

Grace had no idea how long it was after they'd left before she found the courage to open her fingers. The bright kitchen light was reflected by a dozen glittering stone prisms. She shivered, remembering Matthew's eyes. But Matthew's eyes had flamed with passion and anger. The stones she held sparkled coldly, lifelessly.

The single question haunting her was, *why?* Why had she let her doubts about Matthew fester and grow inside her? The answer hurt. It had been her own insecurities, her own fears that had twisted Matthew's love into something dark and ugly.

Vacantly she glanced about her kitchen and wondered where she was going to find the energy to drag herself upstairs. She didn't seem to have the energy to drag herself anywhere.

Christmas came and went. So did New Year's. She spent a lot of time with Jason and tried to make up to him what her terrible foolishness had cost them both. He had been subdued throughout the holidays. And she'd acted irresponsibly by dipping into the money she'd set aside for his college education and overspending on Christmas.

There had been a ski outfit with expensive boots, skis and protective coveralls for him under the tree, along with a television arcade game that had boasted two dozen game cartridges and a snowmobile. She figured she'd spoiled him for a lifetime of Christmases.

Grace had made sure she didn't try to drown her sorrow in work. Jason needed her now more than ever. He was taking Matthew and Brian's disappearance from their lives very hard. So she went skiing with him, lost every single arcade game they played and risked her life every weekend on a speeding snowmobile.

Life went on.

But she didn't know how much longer she could go on. Alone. Without Matthew's love. Grace paced her bedroom. Her tears were for him. She'd hurt him deeply. There was no way he would ever forgive her. What a fool she'd been. A self-absorbed, insecure fool.

She stretched out on her lonely bed. Jason was spending tonight and Sunday with his grandparents. Rolling onto her stomach, Grace hugged her pillow close. Was Matthew alone? Did he ever think of her? Did he hate her?

"Oh, Matthew, I'm so sorry. Please forgive me." Her words fell into the silence of her bedroom, mocking her with their futility.

Impatiently she jumped from her bed. She couldn't bear to remain still for any length of time. She had to do something, anything, to get rid of the nervous energy she could feel gathering inside herself.

Maybe she'd bake something. The first picture that popped into her mind was apple dumplings. Fiercely she rubbed her eyes. She was done crying. No man was worth all the tears she'd cried during the past couple of weeks.

Matthew is, insisted a small voice inside her. He's worth your pride. He's worth whatever it takes to show him that you no longer believe the poison you let fill your mind.

Too late.

Is it?

He'd never forgive her.

Wouldn't he?

It wouldn't be easy. She'd have to catch him alone. Throw herself on his mercy. Beg him to forgive her.

Or seduce him.

Pausing at the shop entrance to Hollister's Auto Repair, Grace didn't even notice the new neatly lettered sign that had replaced its dusty predecessor.

Matthew's father had told her where to find Matthew. She glanced down at her parted coat and found herself looking at pale flesh covered with black lace. She swallowed. Two hours ago in the lingerie department of the local department store, she'd felt fearless about her plans. Now she wasn't so sure. Maybe a grandstand gesture wouldn't appeal to Matthew.

Undecided, she shifted the still-warm dish of apple dumplings she held. Matthew had a particular fondness for her dumplings. But maybe the peekaboo black lace teddy she was wearing under her coat fell in the category of overkill. Grace took three quick breaths. She had the darnedest urge to call out, ready or not, here I come.

Instead she nudged open the swinging doors with her shoulder and stepped into the shop. She spotted a pair of long legs protruding from beneath a dark green car. Well, it was now or never. And she didn't think she could endure never.

"Matthew?"

His legs stiffened momentarily, then he seemed to relax. He said nothing.

"Matthew, I have something I need to tell you."

Metal clanged, and she heard the sound of gurgling liquid.

"Ah, hell."

The mechanic's creeper rolled slowly from beneath the car, and the top half of Matthew came into view. He was wearing a long-sleeved, blue flannel shirt decorated with splotches of oil. He got to his feet, reached automatically for some paper towels and then buried his face in them.

Forever passed as she waited for him to finish wiping his face. Her knuckles whitened as she held onto the dish of dumplings with death-grip tenacity.

Forever ran out when he tossed the blue towels into the trash bin and leveled a lethal glare at her. His face projected no emotion, save perhaps a kind of annoyed curiosity as he eyed the dish she held.

"What do you want to tell me?"

She bit the tender tissue of her bottom lip. "Just that you lied to me."

From his startled expression, Grace could see she'd caught him off guard. Good.

"When did I lie, Grace?" His voice was softly menacing, his eyes darker than the spilled oil that lay at his feet.

"When you told me our love could solve any problem."

"I did say that, didn't I?" He took a step toward her.

"Are you a man of your word?"

"I have a reputation of being so."

"Then you should stand behind what you say. You should be willing to overlook the weaknesses and insecurities of the woman you love."

"Is that what you call your betrayal—weakness and insecurity?"

"Betrayal?"

He nodded slowly. "To yourself and to me. To the life we could have had. To the love we could have shared."

Grace stared at him bleakly. She could feel herself losing hope, losing the spurt of courage and defiance that had spurred her to this reckless confrontation.

"Can you forgive me for doubting you?" There it was, laid out cold and bare.

"Would Blake have forgiven you for doubting him?"

Grace swayed at his cruel bluntness. "You're not Blake."

He moved toward her. "I know. Who am I,

Grace?'' Anger roughened his voice and his features were tautly drawn. ''Say it, damn you.''

Grace flinched. ''You're Matthew Hollister.''

''And what's important to me?''

''Brian,'' she whispered hoarsely.

''And who else?''

''I—I don't know.''

''Yes, you do. Now say it.''

''Ja-Jason?''

''Keep on.''

''Me.'' It was the faintest whisper.

He closed the distance between them. ''Yes, dammit. *You're* important to me. Now tell me the rest of it. You're almost there.''

''The rest of it?''

''*Why* are you important to me?'' he pushed relentlessly.

''Because you love me—for myself. It doesn't matter that I was married to Blake.'' Sunlight broke into all the darkened corners of her heart.

''I love you for yourself.'' He said it as a benediction. ''What's important to you, Grace?''

She smiled, the answer to his question singing inside her. ''Jason and Brian are very important to me. But the most important person in my life is you. I love you, Matthew Hollister.''

''Oh, Lord, I'm glad we got that settled.'' He tried to embrace her and was promptly halted by the covered dish she held. ''What on earth are you holding on to?''

"A peace offering. Will you accept it?"

The corner of his mouth quirked infinitesimally. "That depends. What is it?"

"Homemade apple dumplings."

A wicked gleam appeared in his dark eyes. "You should have said so in the first place. We could have saved some time." He took the dish and peeled back the foil covering it. "I still say they ought to make perfume out of that stuff. No man could resist it." He set the dish of glazed apples on the hood of the car he'd been working on.

Grace gripped the front of her coat, holding it tightly closed. Her apology, the shared honesty and the apple dumplings had worked. Matthew need never know what desperate lengths she would have gone to in order to win him back. He'd never let her live it down if he knew what she was wearing beneath her coat.

"Grace, do you remember when I told you to let go and jump into the future?"

She nodded, aware his manner had suddenly become grave. "I remember."

"I forgot to add that I'd be there to catch you. Come here, darling."

She flew into his arms and clung to him, weeping freely against his shoulder. He stroked her hair.

"It's all right, darling. Don't cry."

"Wh-why not? You are."

He laughed weakly. "So I am. What you do to me, lady." He hugged her tightly to him.

Their lips met, and he claimed her with kisses darkly sweet and fiercely intimate. She felt his hands part her coat, slip beneath it, and then he went absolutely still.

"Good Lord, what on earth have you got on?"

She held her breath, saying nothing.

"Not a whole hell of a lot," he said, answering his own question and taking a step back from her. He gazed at her with shock and desire, then inhaled deeply. "Christmas may have come late, but it did come."

He scooped her up into his powerful arms and carried her from the shop. Grace took secret pleasure from the fact he'd forgotten the dish of dumplings. It was nice to know where she stood in his priorities.

It was when he stopped at his Camaro to open the door for her that Grace spoke again. "Matthew, I know it doesn't really matter, but I want you to know."

"Know what?"

"I've never loved another man as deeply and completely as I love you."

Matthew let her slide to her feet, and his large, callused palms cupped her face. "It matters. I didn't think it did. I didn't think I needed to hear that, but…" His voice broke and it took him a moment to go on. "And you, Grace. I want you to know you stand in no woman's shadow. I love you completely, everlastingly."

Tenderly Grace stroked his sharply chiseled features. "Both of us needed to know."

He captured her fingers and brought them to his lips, kissing them one by one. When he spoke, she could feel his breath against the sensitive pads of her fingertips.

"It's time to go, honey. We've got a future waiting for us."

He opened the car door, but Grace didn't move. They weren't finished. They had to seal the promise with a kiss.

* * * * *

Silhouette —

where love comes alive—online...

eHARLEQUIN.com

your romantic life

—Romance 101—
♥ Guides to romance, dating and flirting.

—Dr. Romance—
♥ Get romance advice and tips from our expert, Dr. Romance.

—Recipes for Romance—
♥ How to plan romantic meals for you and your sweetie.

—Daily Love Dose—
♥ Tips on how to keep the romance alive every day.

—Tales from the Heart—
♥ Discuss romantic dilemmas with other members in our Tales from the Heart message board.

SINTL1R